SAVING
HOPE

Habakkuk

2:2

SAVING
HOPE

S.J. PALMER

LifeRich Publishing is a registered trademark of
The Reader's Digest Association, Inc.

LifeRich Publishing books may be ordered through booksellers or by contacting:

LifeRich Publishing
1663 Liberty Drive
Bloomington, IN 47403
www.liferichpublishing.com
844-686-9607

Editor: Cindy Ray Hale

ISBN: 978-1-4897-4077-9 (sc)
ISBN: 978-1-4897-4076-2 (hc)
ISBN: 978-1-4897-4078-6 (e)

Library of Congress Control Number: 2022904525

LifeRich Publishing rev. date: 03/29/2022

CONTENTS

WRITTEN IN FICTION

Unfortunately, I must tell you that the story written in the pages to come is fiction. Similarities between the characters and real people is accidental . . . mostly. I'll admit, a few of the characters were written to act like someone I know. I'd like to think that all the best characters have a little bit of fact and a little bit of fantasy to them. It helps these characters come to life. Please enjoy the pages that follow as a place that can be built in your heart, and hopefully, you will see it as real in its own special way, just like I do.

DEDICATION

To Dad and Mom who raised me to work for the things I dreamed,

To my siblings who listened to all my ideas,

To all of my grandparents, uncles, aunts and cousins who cheered me on,

To the friends who challenged me to become a better writer,

To God who gave me the words,

This book was not created by my strength alone. Thank you.

Prologue

I RAN LIKE the wind, my feet barely touching the dry crusted ground. My hair caught in the breeze, sweeping over my powerful shoulders. Everything was silent except the thudding of my hooves. The sound resembled a drum. Thump . . . thump . . . thump. . . . Thump . . . thump . . . thump. . . .

The wind gusted slightly, leaves rustling in the breeze. I followed an old trail made by all the animals who walked its surface. Inhaling through my nose, I breathed in the sweet aromas of nature. My home. It had always been the same— steady and true.

I could never have imagined the change coming. I could never have prepared myself for what was about to happen next, but I knew I could do anything one hoof at a time. My heart beat rapidly as it sensed life had changed. For good or bad, I did not know. But I did know one thing: I was Skytears, a mustang, wild and free.

1

A Startling Encounter

THIS SUMMER WOULD not end up like last year. I would make sure of it. It was the last day of school, and freedom had arrived. I had aced all my tests, and my teachers were proud of me. And by teachers, I meant my mom and dad. You see, I was homeschooled, but my parents were not at all easy on me. My mother didn't believe in me being the type of homeschooler who stayed in her pajamas all day. She believed I had a *gifted brain*. So that meant if I flew through a subject in school, I would have another one to take its place immediately. *Learning, how fun.*

But today, everything changed because summer had arrived. I had just sprinted out the door after the last day of school for a long, sunny ride when my mom called after me.

"Hope," she said. "You forgot to muck out the stalls last night, so before you go out gallivanting, you need to clean them." I tried not to moan. *How had I forgotten to clean them?* It seemed to me there was always a stall needing work. But it was way better than staying inside all day, and it would only take a few minutes if I hurried. I ran to the barn.

Only one stall was in use right now because most of the horses stayed in the pastures or in the corral. We had six horses we rode that helped with work on the ranch. There were also a couple dozen other horses we trained and sold or kept for breeding mares. Our horses at Watkins' Wild Ranch, located on the outskirts of Penshaw, Oklahoma, were prized, strong, work horses, and some of them were even rescued mustangs. About fifty years ago, wild horses roamed free on this land we now called home. We named our ranch for its history and added our last name: Watkins.

My horse Chance acted like he still lived on the open range, and I guessed it made sense, since his bloodlines were all mustang. His beautiful, buckskin coat and independent personality reminded me daily of where his roots grew—but I loved him anyway.

His mom was a mustang we'd rescued, and one day, she disappeared. We didn't see her again until one morning, about three months after she disappeared, I walked into the kitchen and almost yelped. The mare had stuck her head in the window and was eating the sugar plum pie my mom had made the day before. Somehow, she had knocked out the protective screen in the window. The mare's name was Sugar, which suited her just fine. Several months later, she had a beautiful colt. So I named him Chance because without his mom accidentally getting out, I wouldn't have him as my wonderful horse.

While I headed for the barn, I heard a tiny bark and glanced over to see my little Australian Shepherd puppy, Wolf, racing beside me. His blue merle fur didn't look like a wolf, but I was hoping he would grow into the name. For now, he was all cuddles and no bite. Mom and Dad decided when I turned fourteen this year, I was old enough to have my own puppy. I couldn't wait to teach him all kinds of tricks and train him to help me with my chores. Right now, though, he just ate and played, which was fine by me. He was undeniably adorable.

I was almost to the barn by now, and Wolf had given up the race and started waddling back to his tiny doghouse on the far side of our house. He was still really young and got tired quickly. I heard a soft, little neigh and turned my attention back to the barn. The call had come from the only horse that currently resided inside the barn: a cute filly named Butterscotch.

When I opened the stall door, Butterscotch nuzzled my pockets looking for treats, knowing that I loved bringing them for the horses. My dad didn't really like it though. He said it spoiled them, but Mom did it too, so there was nothing Dad could do.

Chance must have seen me head into the barn because I heard him whinny. "I'll be there in a second," I called to him. I cleaned the stall out as fast as I could. When I was done, I carefully exited without Butterscotch escaping. The filly was always getting into mischief, so we had to keep a close eye on her. I gave her the carrot I had brought for her and then headed for the fifteen-acre pasture where Chance was.

Closest to the fence was my black Shetland pony, Dash, and sadly, he didn't live up to his name. I had gotten him as a birthday present on my sixth birthday, and he seemed proud of the fact that he was the first horse I'd ever had for my own. He loved to eat and never, *ever* ran. He walked, and at best, trotted. But every little kid loved to name their horse something like Lightning or Flash, so I named him Dash.

I rode Dash until I was eight, and by then, I had really outgrown him. We ended up keeping Dash because he was too cute to give away. Now, eight years after I'd gotten him, he was still no bigger or faster, and he was just as fat. He came up to the fence and started rubbing his nose against my hand, probably looking for food.

The other five horses in the pasture had come closer to Dash and me to see what was happening, including the two my parents rode: a chocolate-brown mare and a dun gelding. Chance walked up to the fence and nipped the other horses like a bad boy as if to tell them, "Hey, back off. She's come to see me."

"Well, aren't you a hot shot," I said with a giggle. I wasn't worried. Chance hadn't really hurt the other horses. I opened the gate, and he trotted through, not needing a halter because he followed me like a dog. This was probably because I was almost always carrying food. Today was not one of those days. Butterscotch had cleaned me out.

I walked into the barn and grabbed the tack for Chance. I also got a brush. After, I put his halter on and tied him loosely to a post. I gave him a good brushing and massage. He moaned contentedly as I groomed him. When I was done, I started to tack him up. As I was putting the saddle pad on him, he snorted.

"Why did you stop brushing me?" he seemed to ask.

"Stop acting lazy," I reprimanded him. Once I had saddled him, I walked Chance to the bridge that crossed the river and ran to the south of the house. He crossed it with ease. Once I had him all the way across, I swung up on him easily and kissed him on the neck. "Good boy," I told him. "Now, let's ride."

We trotted down a path leading to my best friend, Katherine Foster's, house that stretched beyond, branching out in several different directions. I felt at ease here on the trail only Kat and I knew about. The Oklahoma morning was warm, but not scorching, and a slight breeze rustled the grass: a perfect day. The trail was a single-horse dirt path with green trees hanging over it like a tunnel, starting just to the left of the bridge at my house. In the late spring and early summer, the trail was outstandingly gorgeous with green leaves, cool brown soil, and soft short grass. The view gave me hope for what was to come. It was like a sign that this summer would be everything I had dreamed over the last year: three months of adventure, warmth, friendship, and laughter. I clucked to Chance, asking him to trot. He complied, and I began to think on where Kat and I would ride today.

I had brought my saddle bags with two sandwiches and two apples in one bag, and in the other, I had pencils and a sketchbook in case we stopped for a break. I could see an opening in the trail now. Beyond the exit, a seemingly empty pasture sprawled across the open field. I loped Chance around the pasture and past the barn.

Up ahead stood a beautiful wooden house with two stories. I slowed Chance to a smooth walk and glanced around, looking for Kat. I spotted her holding the gate of a big, round pen open. Her dad, John Foster, her brother, Austin, and some of the ranch hands herded about twenty young cattle from the grazing land on the far side of the house into the pasture.

A gust of wind caught Kat's chocolate-colored hair and blew it into her face. When she brought her hand up to push back the strand, I saw the concentration in her ocean-blue eyes. Her usual smile colored her face, the energetic way about her the same as always. When I had talked to Kat on the phone the night before, she had said her family would be moving their stock from the grazing land into a big pen so they could be fattened for the auctions. I guessed it was happening now.

I walked Chance toward the wooden gate—being careful not to scare or get in the way of the cattle—and was about to ask Kat "What's up?" when I heard something. The rattling sound was so terrible it chilled my bones. I glanced down and saw a long grayish-brown creature. My eyes got as big as saucers. I pulled back on the reins, but it was too late. Chance reared and let out a high-pitched cry of alarm. I flew backward, and for a moment, I floated. Then I landed smack down on my back. The air whooshed out of me. There was a pounding sound in my ears.

"Hope," Kat yelled, her voice sounding garbled and weird to my ears. I looked to my left and detected the snake slithering off into the tall grass. *Good*, I thought. By the time Kat got to my side, I had caught my breath and was sitting up. My head was still pounding, but the noise was subsiding.

"Are you okay?" she asked in a panic.

"Yeah," I assured her, getting up and dusting off my pants and shirt. "Where's Chance?" I asked.

"He's fine," Kat told me, pointing to a cowboy who now held Chance's reins. "One of the ranch hands grabbed him when he spooked."

"That was close," I told Kat.

"Hardly," Kat whispered in a panic. An uneasiness showed in her eyes that couldn't have just come from the snake and my rough dismount. "Where did all the cattle go?"

2

Last Summer

I GLANCED AROUND in a panic. Sure enough, all the cattle had disappeared. "Uh . . . oh," I said.

"You can say that again," Kat replied. "We better go see if we can help find them."

"Good idea," I agreed.

As we were walking up to the men, I heard one of them say, "The cattle spooked after the little lady fell."

"They went everywhere, but most of them headed toward the thicket over there," another cowboy said, gesturing across the ranch at a big thick mesh of blackberry vines, flowers, and trees. I had reached the crowd now, and Kat stood right next to me. Someone else had joined the crowd too. Mrs. Elizabeth Foster, who everyone called Liz, was Kat's mom. She was in her late thirties with long blonde hair pulled into a ponytail. Her brown eyes were inviting, like hot chocolate during a winter storm. She was fit to work, but she had a gentle heart.

"I'm sorry I scared the cattle," I told her.

"It wasn't your fault, dear," she said sweetly. "The snake just spooked your horse who spooked the cattle." I felt better after that, but not much. Brushing my own dirty blonde hair out of my face, I looked around at the people. They were all talking amongst themselves, planning what to do next. They weren't focused on Kat and me, which I was relieved to see. None of them seemed mad at me, but they probably weren't happy they now had another thing to deal with. I sighed. This day just took a turn for the worst.

A nagging feeling began in the pit of my stomach. *Was this the beginning of a terrible list of events that would lead to everything falling apart? Would I end up grounded for most of the summer like last year?*

I remembered the betrayal I had felt when Amy Turner, the daughter of my mom's best friend growing up, had deceived me and gotten me a one-way ticket to the worst summer I had ever known. She was supposed to just stay a week, learn about all the wonderful things you could do as a cowgirl. But she wormed her way into the adults' hearts, and when her mother left for home, she somehow managed to convince everyone she should stay for the rest of the summer. Everyone but me, anyway. I'd figured her out almost instantly. She was a chameleon, changing into whatever she needed to get her way.

"Hope," Kat said.

"What?" I asked.

"You know it's rude to ignore your best friend when she's talking to you."

"Sorry. I was lost in thought. What did you say?"

Kat gave me a "what am I going to do with you" face. She repeated herself, "I was just wondering if you were going to need any pain meds. That was a bit of a tumble."

"I'll be fine," I assured her.

"You were thinking about Amy, weren't you?" she asked.

"Yeah," I admitted. "I still can't believe Mom thought she could be my 'summer sister.'"

"She did have almost everyone fooled. But she's not here this year."

I smiled. "And that's why this summer is going to be better. I have a lot of adventure to catch up on."

"I'm right there with ya," Kat said, giving me a hi five.

"You know you weren't grounded, right?"

"But you were grounded from me, which is kind of the same thing."

"True," I said. "Let's not let that happen again."

3

Split Up

MR. FOSTER DECIDED we would split up into groups, each covering a certain stretch of land to find the cattle. The people in my group were Mrs. Liz, Kat, myself, and one other ranch hand who looked to be about seventeen.

"Okay, everyone. Try to be back by dusk," said the Foster's foreman, a sturdy man in his late forties. "Good luck." With that, we split off to get our horses. Once I got to where Chance had been tied, I patted him on the head and unwrapped the reins.

"We're going to go find us some cattle," I told him while I swung into the saddle. I looked over my shoulder and saw Kat coming toward me. She was on a feisty coal-black mare named Calypso.

"You ready?" Kat asked as she came up beside me.

"I'm not very good at herding cattle, but yes, I'm ready," I said.

"Come on, my mom is waiting for us over there." She pointed across the ranch yard, closer to the barn. We trotted over to where Kat's mom stood with the other ranch hand.

"This is Joe, Sundancer, and Banjo," Mrs. Liz said, gesturing to the ranch hand and two horses in turn when we approached. Joe, the red-haired ranch hand, swung up onto Sundancer, a fiery mare with hair as bright as his. Mrs. Liz climbed up onto the big bay she had introduced as Banjo. "Okay, everyone, let's go," Mrs. Liz declared, and we headed off into the trees.

As we were riding, I began to feel nervous. It wasn't really a sound or a glance of something. It was a feeling, a feeling as if someone or something was watching me. *Stop that,* I scolded myself. *You're just imagining it.* I looked around, searching for the cattle and trying to get the weird feeling out of my brain.

Snap.

I glanced around, wildly trying to find the source of the sound.

"Is something wrong, Hope?" Mrs. Liz asked me, concern written in the wrinkles on her forehead.

"Nothing," I replied quickly. I looked to the right. There, behind a bush, I spotted a red-and-white tail. "Look over there," I said, indicating the bush where the steer hid.

"I see him," Joe said as he went around to the other side of the bush.

"Circle him. Make him think he can't run away," Mrs. Liz directed us. We spread out, Kat and me going to the left, Mrs. Liz following Joe around to the right. It turned out that Chance was a natural at herding because he seemed to know exactly how to do something before I did. We circled the steer easily. Since he wasn't scared anymore, he calmly walked in the middle, knowing we were taking him back to where he belonged.

We had ridden a minute or two when Mrs. Liz said, "We can take him the rest of the way back. You girls go and see if you can find any more of the cattle." She turned to her daughter. "Kat, check over in the meadow with the blueberries."

"Okay, Mom," Kat replied.

"Make sure not to separate," Mrs. Liz instructed us.

"We won't," Kat and I said in unison.

"Here, take my phone just in case. Joe's number is programmed in there," she said, handing the phone to Kat. "Be careful." With that, they rode off.

"Okay," Kat declared. "Follow me. The meadow is this way."

As we were riding, Kat began talking about how she had been riding one day out in the grazing land and stumbled across a baby mountain lion. She had been scared, not because of the baby cougar, but because the mother could have been anywhere. She could have been stalking Kat at that moment. Thankfully, the little energetic cougar hadn't spotted her, so she'd carefully backed Calypso up and eased back up the trail. Arriving home, she'd told her dad, and he'd said if the cougars caused any trouble, he would call the wildlife department to come and move the cats to a different area. For now, though, they were fine where they were.

Kat brought up another topic, but I wasn't listening. I had lost myself in thought, reliving the fear I had felt when I'd woken up late one night in the middle of summer to find Chance missing.

"And I've lost her again," Kat said.

"Who in their right mind would take another girl's horse?" I asked aloud, bringing Kat into my train of thought. This wasn't the first time we had discussed the incident, so Kat jumped in with no problem.

"A crazy person," she said. "Though I admit, I've dreamed of riding around with wild mustangs at night myself, too."

"I still can't believe I got in trouble for trying to help Chance escape from a madwoman." I crossed my arms. I could still feel the embarrassment of being chewed out by both my parents. They had been livid.

"You knew the rule. No riding after dark by yourself. But you ignored it and chased after Amy in the middle of night on one of the mares your family had just gotten tamed. She was a skittish wreck for four months after that."

"But it was to save Chance," I said, patting his neck.

"You should have gotten your parents first," Kat said, repeating the line I had heard nearly a hundred times last summer.

"Whose side are you on?"

"Yours," Kat said. "I don't want you to have to take summer school again—or do more chores."

"Or lose Chance again too," I agreed. Kat stared me down for a solid eight seconds before I amended, "I couldn't stand another summer without you, either."

"Well, I'm glad I was missed." We both laughed.

"At least Amy got sent home after that," I said. "Imagine getting grounded with her for the summer."

"Your parents wouldn't have done that to you, would they?" Kat asked.

"It was entirely possible. They are really creative with punishments. They say it helps with character development."

We settled into a relaxed quiet. But it only lasted a few minutes. The creepy feeling was back again. At one point, I thought I caught a glimpse of white out of the corner of my eye. But then it was gone. Another time, all was quiet then. . . .

Crunch.

I swiftly glanced around, looking for the cause of the sound. Nothing.

"You okay?" Kat asked.

"Fine," I replied, somewhat shaky.

"Are you sure?" Kat asked me, concern creeping into her voice. I took a deep, slow breath.

"Yes, I'm sure," I replied more firmly.

"Well, we're almost there anyway," Kat said. We had come to a flat stretch of land by now. "Race you to the woods over on the other side," she yelled. And with that, she kicked Calypso, and they sped off.

"Hey, you had a head start," I yelled after her and laughed. I kicked Chance and gave him his lead, and then we were chasing after them. "Chance was always faster," I called as we pulled up beside them. Calypso squealed in defiance.

"You're right, girl," Kat told her horse. "Let's show them." They dashed ahead.

In the end, Chance and I won, but Kat declared, "You two had an unfair head start." She laughed.

"Yeah, right," I exclaimed, grinning from ear to ear. We arrived at the valley about five minutes later. As we came out of the forest we had been traveling in, my eyes swept the valley below: no cattle.

"I don't see any cattle," Kat said, reading my mind. "But they might be behind something where we can't see them. Let's go look."

"Okay," I replied. "I'll go to the right. You go to the left."

She agreed, and we started down the hill into the valley.

The valley was warm and bright. Everything was in full bloom, green and luscious. Flowers of all shapes, colors, and sizes were vibrant and healthy. The May weather was perfect. When I got down to the bottom, everything was quiet; no birds chirped, no frogs croaked in the pond on the other side of the valley.

Then it happened. Chance quivered beneath me, or at least, I thought it was him at first. But the shuddering became much too violent for a horse to make. I noticed pebbles cascading down a short cliff off to the far side of the valley. The flowers began to shake fervently, and I heard Chance let out a short grunt of surprise, and maybe a little panic. My brain was in slow-mo. *What is going on?* An alarmed whinny broke my haze. No horse I knew made that same sound. It sounded sharp and high-pitched, like the sound a fiddle makes when the musician let the bow slip and an extra note rang out off-key. I glanced around, trying to pinpoint where the sound had come from.

Crack.

There was a loud rumbling sound, then a squeal of alarm from the mysterious creature. I started to panic. I had to help the poor animal.

"Come on, Chance. We have to hurry," I told him as I urged him toward the place where I heard the sounds. We rounded the corner of a gigantic boulder, and I gasped. What I saw in front of me was terrible.

About twenty feet ahead, a gorgeous, dappled-gray mare lay on her side. Her leg was wedged between an old log and a massive rock. She tried her best to struggle free but had no leverage. The mare's eyes were the worst part. They were white with terror and confusion. She squealed again sadly, desperately trying to get up but falling again. Soon the mare might get hurt even worse. I had to get her free.

4

Nice And Easy

THE MARE WAS calming down a bit, but I knew she could be going into shock, hopefully not. Taking several deep breaths to calm myself, I prayed to God for wisdom. Nothing immediately came to me, but I did feel a little less overwhelmed.

"Easy," I whispered to Chance as I gently tugged back on the reins for him to stop. Once he halted, I quietly slid to the ground. I led him to the nearest small tree and tied him to it. He could ground tie, but I didn't want him to spook if the mare tried to bolt. "Be a good boy and stay quiet," I whispered to him. I began moving toward the frightened and injured mare.

She nickered questioningly as if to ask, "Who are you? Please don't hurt me."

Wanting to soothe her, I answered in a soft voice, "Don't worry. I'm not going to hurt you. I'm a friend." I was six yards away now, and the mare hadn't moved yet. She was watching me carefully, but she seemed to understand I wasn't a threat, at least I hoped so. As I reached the mare, I crouched down slowly, trying to figure out how to help her.

One of the mare's delicate legs was wedged between a large rock and an old tree trunk. As I got a better look, I could see the leg being smashed was the left back. I looked around for something to pry the mare's leg out from between the log and the massive rock. The only thing around was a tree branch that must have fallen down when the last storm blew in a couple of days ago. It was light and strong. *Perfect*, I thought.

"Okay, this will probably hurt for just a second, and then it will be all better," I whispered to the mare. I wedged the branch in between the rock and the log, beside the mare's leg. "Okay, on three. One . . . two . . . three. . . ." I shoved down on the branch. For a moment, nothing happened. I pressed down with all my might, but neither the rock nor the log moved. When my arms were about to give out, there was a crack, and the log toppled off the mare's leg.

I backed away as the mare stumbled to her feet. She took a few waddling paces away using three legs, and I turned back to Chance and started walking toward him. I always carried my saddlebags when trail riding. *Please be in there.*

Please be in there. I reached Chance and patted him on the neck.

"Good boy." I lifted the flap of the saddlebag. I noticed nothing useful, just my sketchpad and pencils. I went around to the right side and opened it. There, below my snacks, was a small emergency kit. I reached in the bag and brought out the kit. I grabbed my canteen as well. I started back to the mare, but she shied.

"Easy, girl. This will help," I crooned. I tried again to approach her, and again, she shied. "It's okay, this will help," I reassured as calmly as I could. My heart was about to beat out of my chest, but I needed to stay calm for the mare.

This time, she allowed me to approach just a little. I decided I had better get what I needed out of the emergency kit and leave the rest behind. No doubt, the beautiful mare would not allow the clumsy, creaky, red box beside her, especially when her most powerful weapon was injured and unusable. I quietly bent down and slowly opened the kit.

Inside, I fumbled around, trying to find something useful to help the poor mare. There was some gauze wrap and a little peroxide—not much, about a half of a cup. It would have to act as disinfectant. I pocketed the gauze wrap and grabbed the peroxide, closing the first aid kit quietly.

Rising slowly, I inched toward the mare, who was now probably seven feet away. The mare pricked her ears forward, ready to detect anything that might be a danger to her. I inched closer. The mare didn't move. I inched closer, and the mare was silent. Before long, I was about four feet away. I took a deep breath to calm myself, worried the mare might be able to sense how scared I was. I inched a foot, then another foot. Now I was a mere two feet away. I gulped. If the mare bolted, she would be gone, and I could do nothing.

"Easy, girl," I stammered. "It's okay." I slowly reached out my free, trembling hand. The mare's body was soft, silky, and the warmest, most comfortable thing I had ever felt. The mare didn't flinch. The only thing showing the mare was alive was her skin rippling and shivering gently beneath my hand whenever I touched her shoulder. Her leg probably wasn't broken, but the cut left from the tree was enormous.

"Okay, girl," I whispered. "I'm going to put this liquid on your leg. It's going to sting for just a second." I poured a little into my hand. "I'm going to count to three again. One . . . two . . . three. . . ." I comforted the mare while reaching out with my hand and gently rubbing the peroxide on her leg. She neighed skittishly and shifted away from me. "Easy. . . ." I soothed.

I started to unwrap the gauze. There was nothing to cut it with, so I just ripped it. The mare nickered softly and twisted her head around to watch me. I gently patted her injured leg and slowly wrapped the gauze around it. The mare grunted but allowed me to continue wrapping. If I'd been a little taller or louder, the mare likely wouldn't have allowed me in her presence. It was surprising I had gotten this far. She either knew I was no threat, or she was more injured than I thought. I twisted the gauze a certain way so it would not come off, hopefully.

"That will have to do," I told the mare, rising slowly. "You're a brave girl," I praised her, putting my right hand on the mare's side. She shifted herself away from me so she was facing me, and I could no longer touch her.

"Hope," a familiar voice yelled. I spun my head around. Kat stood a little way off, gawking at where the mare stood behind me. I turned around to the mare, but she started to back up nervously. She turned and loped off into the thicket. Even keeping most of her weight off the injured leg, her movements were graceful and quiet. She seemed to move with the shadows created by the trees and foliage, a ghost of a horse, disappearing as quickly as she had appeared.

5

Nightmare

I SCREAMED AND shot up in bed. My heart pounded a skittering beat in my chest, and my legs and arms flailed, trying to escape the confines of my covers. It took me a few panicked moments to realize I was in my room, not with the mysterious mare who had been in an earthquake and gotten pinned beneath a fallen tree. After the mare had run off, Kat and I had returned to her ranch. All the cattle had been rounded up by the time we returned. The rest of the day returned to normal. But the night was a different story. Three days later, I was still reliving the awful sound of the mare's cry of terror. It came to me every night.

What if the mare's wound got infected? What if it inhibited her ability to move? I knew of several wild animals in these parts who would prey on the slow and weak. Sitting here, thinking about it the past couple of days, had been driving me crazy. I needed to find out what had happened to her. It seemed a nearly impossible task, considering how much open land there was where I lived. *But even if I manage to find her again, is there anything I can do? Or is it too late already?*

My mind went into panic mode, and I slipped back into my nightmare.

"Rain," I called softly, then more loudly, "Come here, girl. Raindancer." That was what I had decided to call the mare, because she looked like rain after a long drought. I looked around me. For some reason, I couldn't see anything. It was like I was in an ocean, thousands of feet below the surface, an alarming void that could never be penetrated.

I heard a whinny. Then, in front of me, the mare appeared. She was gorgeous. Her form swirled in and out of focus like a mist or cloud. I just stared at her, spellbound. But then she suddenly evaporated into wisps that floated back into the darkness. My eyes scoured the expanse, but she had vanished without a clue to her presence. The dream left me dizzy and scared. I had to remind myself what was really happening. I looked up. Everything was completely normal.

My tall, black bookcase stood across the room from me, my favorite spot in the house. Horse figurines and other statuettes stood on different parts of the shelves, guarding all the treasures residing there. Like always, the sight helped to calm me.

I kicked off the covers and swung my legs around the side of the bed. Getting up, I walked to the bathroom. After brushing my teeth, hair, and changing into some comfortable jeans and a soft blue T-shirt, I walked downstairs to get something to eat and to try to escape my nerves for the lost mare.

I swiftly finished eating and couldn't stand just thinking about it any longer. Sprinting up the stairs, I dashed into my room and picked up the phone on my desk. Mom and Dad had said I couldn't have a phone until I was fifteen, but they had given me a home phone to keep in my room—it was even my favorite shade of blue—so it was a good start. I dialed Kat's phone. Her parents had heard about what my mom and dad had done and thought it was a good idea, so Kat had a phone in her room too. After five rings I was beginning to think that no one was going to answer when a man's voice called over the phone, "Hello. May I ask who's calling?" I recognized the speaker as Kat's dad.

"Hey, this is Hope. I was wondering if Kat was around," I asked.

"Yes, she is," came his reply. "Kat, Hope is on the phone, and she wants to talk to you," I heard him call out. There was the *click* of someone picking up the phone and the *click* of someone putting the other phone down.

"Hello," came Kat's voice a moment later.

"Hey, Kat. It's Hope," I said.

"What's up? What did you want to talk to me about?" Kat asked.

"Well, I was wondering if you wanted to go riding after you get all your chores done, just for fun?" I questioned, not yet telling her the real reason for going riding.

"I'd love to go riding just for some fun, but that's not the only reason, is it?" Kat asked, probably already knowing the answer. She knew me all too well.

"Well . . . " I said slowly, not sure she would like the idea. "I wanted to go and see if we could find the mare and check if she's still hurt or if she's healing. I really want her to be okay. What if she is hurt or crippled or something? We have to find her," I said all of this in one quick breath, without any space in between the words.

"Sounds great," Kat replied. I breathed a sigh of relief. She wanted to go with me. "What time do you think we should go?"

"As soon as we can be ready," I told her.

"Okay, I can be ready in about two hours. How about you?" she asked. I glanced sideways at my clock on my dresser. It was 7:45 a.m.

"Let's try to meet in the little opening between our houses beside the secret trail at ten o'clock."

"Good idea," she said, "Well, we better get working. See you in a little bit. Bye."

"Bye," I repeated. I heard the *click* of her hanging up. Setting the phone down, I went downstairs and outside, eager to finish the chores.

Two hours later, I was pacing the barn, trying to think of something I had forgotten to do. At this rate, Kat would be waiting on me to finally arrive. I had fed and watered the chickens, collected the eggs, watered the horses, and given them their hay.

During the summer, there was plenty of grass in their pastures. They only got grain in the winter or on a special occasion. I freshened up Butterscotch's stall and gave her some milk and a little grain. She would be weaned in a few weeks, but for now, I fed her a mix of the two foods. Wolf had also been fed and watered. He was now savoring the leftover pork we had eaten last night. I couldn't think of anything I hadn't done. I walked to the house, opened the door, and poked my head in. "Hey, Mom?"

"Yes, honey," she answered as she walked to the front door. She was wearing a yellow T-shirt and jeans with her hair pulled up into a messy bun.

"Can I go ride with Kat now?" I asked.

"Have you done all your chores?" she questioned.

"Yes."

She looked at me, unbelievingly curious. "List them," she challenged, folding her arms.

I did, and she smiled.

"Well, I guess you can but be back before dinner."

"I will," I promised. I hugged her and sprinted out the door. I ran up to the barn to get the saddle. I carried it and a bridle as quickly as I could to the fence of the pasture Chance stayed in. Reaching it, I slung the saddle up onto the fence and called out, "Here, Chance. Come here, boy."

I heard the "heartbeat of the ranch" as my Grandpa always called it: the horse hooves running across the ground. Looking to the hill, I saw the shape of Chance appear over the crest. He reared up, his head stretched to the sun as if to touch it. Then down his head went as he kicked up his heals, bolting down the hill toward me.

It wasn't hard to imagine him as a majestic stallion with a herd of his own. I knew in my heart he actually had a herd. It was a family of just me and the other saddle horses, but still a family. I think he liked that just fine. I walked up to the fence and jumped onto it, reaching out to pat him on his forehead. His velvety face pressed up against my hand, asking for more.

"Good boy," I told him. I eased the bridle over his head and into place. Then I got the saddle and hauled it over to Chance and placed it on his strong back. After making sure everything was secure, I led him through the gate out of the pasture. A rule Dad had always enforced here at our ranch was if a gate was open, leave it open. If the gate was closed, leave it closed or go through it if you needed to and close it behind you.

I securely locked it after I had gotten an impatient Chance and myself through the gate. As a last-minute thought, I grabbed my saddlebags and attached them to Chance's gear. The saddlebags held all of my regular necessities, plus a few things I added on the fly.

I had clean rags and antibiotics for rudimentary first-aid. A small rope had been included in case anything needed to be held in place. I doubted the mare would let the rope get close to her, but I'd rather be overprepared than the alternative. My canteen was filled with water, and I had stuffed some beef jerky into the saddlebags as well. Lastly, I had packed a camera, just in case.

I jumped up on Chance as gracefully as a swan swims in water. I was *so* ready for today. This was what I was born to do. I leaned down next to Chance's ear and kissed him on the neck. "Come on, boy. We don't have all day. Let's ride."

6

A Search

A FEW MOMENTS later, I raced Chance through the secret trail. Leaves hung in the middle of the path and slapped at my face occasionally, but I didn't mind it much. My mind was racing ahead of Chance's hoof beats. *Where should we start looking? Has the mare moved a whole lot in the few days since I've seen her?* I hoped not. I wanted to make sure she was okay, and her moving off meant it would be much harder for me to find her. Chance's hooves ate up the ground, so much so, that we were rounding the last bend in this part of the trail now. Off to the left, a smaller trail curved back and forth for about 500 yards. At the end of the almost invisible trail, was a little opening. It was about the size of a regular round pen for working horses. Kat wasn't here yet, giving me a little time to figure out the plan.

First, we would go back to where I had seen Raindancer. Second, if we found her, we would inspect her leg—if she was in a good mood and let us get close to her, of course. Our chances weren't great, but we had to try.

Chance pranced in place, throwing his head up and letting out a happy nicker like he was ready for the adventure. Another whinny harmonized with his. I knew by the sweet sound of the call, it had come from Calypso. They had to be close. A few moments later, I spotted them entering the opening. Kat smiled when she saw me.

"You always have to be the first person here, don't you," she said, more like a fact than a question. I laughed at her comment.

"It gives me time to think," I explained. Calypso trotted up to Chance, and they nuzzled noses as if they were whispering to each other, talking about all the latest gossip.

"So, are you ready to find the mare?" Kat asked. I looked straight into her excited eyes.

"Yes. I'm a little nervous, though," I told her.

"That's okay. You have nothing to worry about," she promised. "Nothing bad ever happens when I'm on the job." She stuck out her chest and held her head dramatically high. I busted into a fit of giggles. She always managed to make me feel better.

"Right. Nothing *ever* happens," I agreed. We both knew that sometimes Kat brought craziness around with her. It was a good thing we weren't close enough for her to punch me

31

because she probably would have attempted it. "Okay, let's get moving," I said while holding back my laughter.

I gave Chance his lead, and we trotted off, leaving Kat and Calypso behind us. I heard more horse's hooves behind me. Kat was still giggling. I smiled, remembering when I had told Kat about what happened to the mare before she had arrived.

Kat assured me she was going to help in any way possible, and I knew she meant it wholeheartedly. We had decided our first step was to search the place I had seen the mare. I hoped more than anything we would be able to help the mare. She could be crippled, limping; her leg could be infected or worse. She could be alone and cold, maybe even . . . *Stop it. You are accomplishing nothing by worrying. Philippians 4:6. Don't worry about anything, but in everything, through prayer and petition with thanksgiving, present your requests to God.* I recited the verse Mom had taught me recently. Knowing what a worrywart I usually was, the verse felt specifically targeted at me. I sent up a quick prayer as well, asking for the mare's safety.

Then I tried to think of something else. I focused on the trail and the leaves and the grass. My gaze drifted to the squirrels in the trees, such small and curious creatures. Before I knew it, we were on top of the hill overlooking the valley. At first, I saw nothing. Then, as my eyes swept the woods behind the meadow, I caught a glimpse of white, and then I heard the steady rhythmic thumping of a horse's hooves. It was quiet, but definitely there. I detected another patch of white farther to the left, then farther down, I saw another white flicker. The sound got steadily louder.

All at once, I saw her, trotting slowly and quietly, her head down. She came out into the clearing, and I stifled a gasp. The mare seemed perfectly fine, not at all like what I had thought. She looked unaffected by her injured leg, though I couldn't see clearly from this distance. As I was watching her, the mare did something I didn't except. Her elegant head went up, she tested the air, and then she turned her head toward the woods and let out a whinny.

I glanced over at Kat to see what she thought of the mare's actions. She was sitting perfectly still, her eyes transfixed on the mare with awe and wonder. Before I could ask what Kat thought about Rain's actions, leaves rustled loudly, twigs snapped, and drums thumped. My head swung back to Rain. *Drums?* My jaw dropped.

7

Lesson Learned

AM I IN heaven? Have I died? Because what I saw in front of me was only something I had seen in my dreams. I sat in shock, unable to do anything but breathe. It wasn't drums I had heard. It was the sound of a dozen wild horses. In front of me were about seven mares, four foals, and a fierce stallion. He trotted up to Rain and nipped at her viciously. Although he seemed to want to be in command, he didn't look like he could've been that old. His stature resembled that of a two or three-year-old at most. He had grown to what I assumed was his full size, but he had not filled out in a way that showed maturity, which meant he couldn't have started this herd. Even though he seemed to be strong and swift, I doubted he had won these mares from other stallions. I could be wrong, but I doubted it.

His coat gleamed darkly in the sunlight, the color of molten gold. His mane, tail, and the bottom of his legs contrasted beautifully and seemed to soak into the shadows. I would usually think comparing a real mustang to an animated cartoon would be silly, but this horse looked exactly like Spirit. This mustang was the life-size version of *The Stallion of the Cimarron*. I mentally named him after the movie right then and there. I glanced around at the other horses: blacks, bays, pintos, and paints. My mind went back to Rain. She had come here, tested the wind, and then called the band to her. My heart skipped a beat. She wasn't just a wild mustang. She was the boss mare of a band of wild horses.

"Wow. . . ." Kat whispered beside me. I nodded slowly, still trying to process what I was seeing. Suddenly, Chance bolted. I clung to his neck, trying desperately not to fall off. He was running up to the other horses. He slowed to a trot, but my heart had started to pound double-time now.

Kat cried out, "Hope, get out of there." I knew what she meant. Chance was acting stupid. He saw more horses and had to go say hi. But he forgot one thing.

The stallion blew out his nose and stomped the ground. Thump . . . thump . . . thump. . . . The message was clear. "Watch it, buddy. You're on my turf." But apparently, Chance didn't get the message. He trotted up closer toward the stallion. *Big mistake.* Spirit charged. His head was down, his eyes murderous. He was probably fifty yards away, but he would be on top of us in a matter of seconds.

I kicked Chance into a full out, fleeing gallop, turning him around back toward home. He gladly ran his heart out. We quickly passed Kat's fleeing mare. Kat was clinging to Calypso, but since they weren't the ones who'd angered the stallion and neither of them was another threatening male, they were probably safe. Chance was the fastest horse I knew of in these parts, but Spirit was a wild stallion protecting his herd. We were in a losing battle if Spirit continued the charge. I risked a quick glance over my shoulder. Spirit turned back to his herd and tossed his head, like he was proud to have saved his band. I slowed Chance just enough for Kat's mare to catch up. Once she did, I loosened Chance's reins, and we galloped all the way back home.

I had learned my lesson; *never* let your gelding go crazy and run up to the mares of a stallion's herd. As we were rounding the final bend in the secret passage, I slowed Chance to a trot. After a minute, I pulled him to a stop. Behind me, Calypso's hooves dug into the ground as Kat halted her as well. Calming my breathing to a normal rate, I turned Chance to face Kat.

"Let's not tell anyone what just happened, okay?" I asked Kat.

"Probably a good idea," she agreed. I nudged Chance into a walk, aiming for Kat's house. It would not take us long to reach her place from here.

I made a shame-on-you humming noise and placed my hands on my hips. "Chance, what got into you? You are smarter than this. Never do anything like that again."

Chance nickered. I took it to mean, "Oh, come on. Did you see all of the cute mares?"

"Knock it off. Okay, Chance? They weren't yours for the taking." I pulled him to a halt. "You sure made the stallion mad." We had reached the opening behind Kat's house. Calypso came up beside Chance and snorted at him, probably telling him he needed to behave better next time.

"I'll call you tonight, okay?" Kat inquired.

"Okay," I agreed. "Bye." She smiled and waved, then trotted Calypso down the path leading to her family's ranch. I turned Chance toward ours and urged him into a trot. After reaching home, I cooled Chance off, untacked him, brushed him down, and put him back into the pasture. I went into the house and gobbled down some food. It was a little bit past one o'clock in the afternoon. Tired and worn out from the day, I trudged upstairs to take a quick nap. Running from a crazy jealous mustang was tiring. Walking into my room, I fell onto my bed in a heap. My eyes closed instantly, and minutes later, sleep overtook my body.

8

Another Option

THE GROUND RUMBLED. I bolted but wasn't quick enough. The branch came crashing down. Pain flared like fire up my foreleg, and I cried out in pain. I tried to scramble up to my feet, but I couldn't. My front hooves kept slipping and sliding. My left back leg felt like it was being ground into dirt. Fear like I had never known lanced through me. A groan escaped me. I was in terrible trouble.

My eyes opened, and my strong head shot up. Around me, everything was quiet, and I let out a long breath. Getting up, I stretched and shook my whole body, prancing in place, trying to work the stiffness out of my legs. I swung my head around. None of the other members of the herd had awakened yet. They all slept soundly. Most of them would not be rousing for a while. It was still dark; the sun wouldn't be up for about an hour.

I began picking my way around the herd, careful not to trip over any young foals who slept on the ground or run into any of the other members who slept standing up. Weaving through them, I trotted over to the spot where The General stood. He went to sleep after all the other members did and was the first one up. He took care of his herd. It was his duty, and he would not let any creature touch a hair on any of the members of his family.

As I got closer, I could make out his shape against the pale moonlight. He stood strong and graceful. For a moment, I remained there, not wanting to break the peaceful quiet of the early morning. The General was not the strongest stallion or the biggest, but he was the fastest, wisest, most graceful, and kindest one who would do anything for the members of his herd. I looked up to him and hoped I could be strong and gentle at the same time like him one day. I dipped my head and quietly asked, "Would you like me to keep watch and let you rest, Father?" He let out a tired breath.

"I would," he replied in a low voice. He pressed his muzzle briefly against mine in thanks. "Wake me if anything seems strange." He walked off to go rest with the mares and youngsters while I stood and watched the herd. No one said anything about my father's age, but we all knew he was past his prime and got tired more quickly. We all helped him in little ways, not wanting to hurt his pride. My father was just not as young as he once was. All the other stallions were younger, bigger, and stronger. Soon my father would need to choose his successor to take over his herd.

I wanted to believe I could take over his herd, but that was impossible. A stallion must lead. Since my momma died last season, I had become the boss mare. I knew the land. My momma had taught me all she knew about the wild. I would do my best, but no one could lead like she had. I wasn't the official boss mare, probably because I was younger than most and didn't have as much experience. It just kind of happened.

Even if it wasn't official, I was doing my best to take care of the herd. I shook myself out of my thoughts. If I wasn't careful, I could lose myself in thought and space out, which would not help to take care of my family. Nothing was going to hurt the herd while I was on watch.

The night was quiet. The only sound was the rustling of the leaves and the occasional cry of a coyote in the distance. As the dawn began to rise, coloring and bringing warmth to the land, my thoughts wandered again. I began thinking of who would take my father's place. Other stallions roamed the nearby lands, but none I really liked. Most were too young or already had their own herds farther away. Only one option came to mind. I shivered involuntarily.

Magma. Headstrong, bossy, arrogant Magma. He would have been my last choice, but sadly, no other opponents seemed as realistic. Usually, my father would've told any foal of his it was time to strike out on their own by this time. But in my father's old age, he had grown sentimental, especially since we were the last foals our mother had. But Magma was my least favorite brother. We were so different.

He was aggressive and brash. I was inquisitive and thoughtful. He boasted, and I worked to do my best. He had a dark buckskin coat and pitch-black mane, tail, and stockings, similar to our father's but much more extreme. I had a gray-blue-white speckled coat like our mother's. He was older than me but only by a few minutes. The herd had been surprised when my mother had two foals. It was rare, and usually one of us would have been too weak and died, but I think we were both too stubborn to be the weaker one. So, we both grew up strong.

Sometimes I wished there was another option for herd stallion other than Magma, maybe Fleetfoot. *No. Impossible. Fleetfoot is gone.* He would have been an amazing herd leader, with his pitch-black coat and strong but gentle aura that filled you with energy. Everyone overlooked him because of his tentativeness and swift gaits. I was one of the few who knew he wasn't really scared, just cautious. Not the boldest, but maybe, the smartest. If he was still here, he would be a young and spunky but wise two-year-old. But he wasn't.

He had died as a yearling. No one had actually seen his body, but there had been an earthshake and massive trees had fallen. Birds flew, leaves swirled with no pattern, small animals scattered in a whirlwind of fur, heaps of debris and foliage were everywhere. By the time it was over, many of us were injured, some major, others minor, but Fleetfoot . . . Fleetfoot was gone, nowhere to be found. His mother Moonlace had been heartbroken. She had been out in the wild by herself. Moonlace had been the only one of her herd to escape a gathering.

Gatherings happened without warning, and many herds couldn't fight them. The two-legs would rush in and take those they could catch. No horse ever saw the ones who were caught ever again. Moonlace wandered alone until my father found her and brought her to the safety of the herd. A week later she had Fleetfoot. My mother once told me that even though he wasn't my father's son, he still loved Fleetfoot like his own.

Fleetfoot had been my best friend, and he was gone. We searched and searched but to no avail. My closest companion was gone forever. Some parts of me still thought there was a chance he had survived. *But wouldn't he have come back? Why had we not found him?* Shivering, I shook the images out of my head. There was nothing to be done. We would never see him again.

9

New Adventure

MONDAY MORNING BROUGHT loads of clouds and rain, which was a good thing for the grass. Still, it meant no riding out with Kat. I sat in a chair by the only window in my room, looking out into the pasture as the horses ran across the spongy earth, reveling in the coolness that the rain brought them. I smiled, wishing I was outside with them. Mom had said it was still too cold to play in the rain, so I had to stay inside. On the bright side, it also meant I got time to sit and read in my pajamas for half the day. I would just have to ride double tomorrow.

I was deep in my latest mystery novel when I heard a knock at my door. I looked up to see black hair and a handsome face with hazel eyes the same color as mine. "I brought pizza home from town for dinner," Dad said.

"Really?" I asked, smiling.

He laughed. It was loud and a little boyish, and I liked it. "Really."

We headed downstairs where Mom had set out our plates and laid the two Tony's Pizza Palace pizza boxes, cheese and pepperoni, both with triple cheese added on. I thanked my parents for the food, and then we ate in comfortable silence for a minute. I was grabbing my third slice when I looked up to see my mother smiling at me. Dad was trying to hide his expression behind a mouthful of pizza.

Now my mom was almost always smiling, but there was something different about it this time. "What's up?" I asked. Her smile grew even bigger.

"You know your cousin, Riley? Well, she and I were on the phone the other day, and she was telling me about a summer camp she went to last year."

"Yeah," I said, not really sure where this conversation was headed.

"Well, it's called Cowboy Camp and is held at the Walden Creek Ranch in Wolford, Oklahoma," she said. "The camp allows teenagers to spend time with their friends out in the mountains."

"That sounds cool," I responded, slightly interested.

"You bring your horse too," Dad added, sharing a knowing look with Mom. "That's one of the main events at camp—learning more about your horse and how to do all sorts of cool stuff." Mom began to list all the different aspects of camp which included canoeing, river rafting, hiking, and group activities, all while staying in cabins that had less than great air conditioning units and tiny bathrooms. I jumped up from my seat, the incredible pizza entirely forgotten.

"That sounds amazing," I gasped.

"Good," Mom said and laughed, "because we already signed you up. I talked to Kat and Austin's parents, and they are going too."

"Aaaaahhhhhh," I squealed, jumping like a penguin on hot coals. My parents both smiled at me, obviously pleased I was so excited. Just then, the phone rang. I dashed to it and looked at the number. Seizing the phone, I screamed into it. "We're going to Cowboy Camp."

I heard the squeals of excitement escaping Kat's mouth on the other end. "I can't believe it," she gasped.

"I know," I squealed again. "It's official. This is going to be the best summer ever." I had to remember to thank Riley later. She was the best cousin I could have.

That week, I didn't think about Rain much. I was too busy getting ready for Cowboy Camp. I would be leaving the following Sunday afternoon. Today was Monday, so it meant I had a lot to do before we left. The barn needed to be thoroughly cleaned out, and the tack room needed to be organized. Mom said my room had to be "spotless—every nook and cranny."

All the water troughs needed to be dumped out, scrubbed, and refilled. I needed to pack my clothes, Chance's tack, his grooming supplies, and snacks for me. Dad also suggested I take Dash. There were some younger kids coming for several days who would absolutely adore him. Dad also hinted I would need Dash for something else at Cowboy Camp, but I wasn't sure what. I also had to clean out the chicken coops.

Working hard all week, my excitement built up and up until I was sure I would burst. Saturday evening after dinner, I was grooming Chance and Dash really well so their coats shimmered in the sun. I wanted them to look extra special for tomorrow. The plan was for me to have everything packed up in my dad's truck tonight, so when we went to church in the morning we were driving straight to Kat's house. We would load up the tack from our truck and the horses into Mr. Foster's trailer and go to camp from there. I would be riding Chance and ponying Dash over to the Foster's tonight so all the horses would have a chance to get acquainted before camp. Kat was going to ride me back to my house from there.

After I finished grooming Chance to perfection, I bridled him and swung on. Since his tack was already loaded, I would be riding Chance bareback tonight. I didn't ride Chance without a saddle often because it was cumbersome to carry anything, but I also enjoyed getting to ride like this sometimes. I leaned over and unwrapped Dash's lead rope. Riding out of the barn I hollered, "Be back in about forty-five minutes."

"Okay, be careful," Dad hollered back from one of the horse pastures. Clucking, I eased Chance into a brisk walk toward Kat's house. The trip was peaceful and beautiful as the sky began to change to an orange sunset. Before I knew it, I was passing the Fosters' first pasture, then the paddock, then I was pulling up to their barn.

"Hey, stranger," came a familiar voice. I glanced over my shoulder to see Austin Foster striding across the yard from the house.

He had grown taller during the school year, about two inches taller than me—five-foot-six, I guessed. His short blond hair and bright blue eyes were the same as always. Some days, I thought Kat looked a lot like her older brother, but then other days, he wore that half smile full of mischief, making him look entirely all his own.

"Where's Kat?" I asked him.

"Had to do a last-minute shopping run with Mom," he replied.

"Oh," I said. "What'd she forget?"

"She forgot to tell Mom she was out of shampoo and toothpaste," Austin said. "Plus, Mom had forgotten that Kat's swimsuit hadn't made it through last summer. You know how the women in my family are."

"Severe underpackers," I said, stifling a laugh. *Packing light was a skill, but not when you forgot cornerstone pieces like toothpaste and pajamas.*

"They'll be back in about an hour or so," he said.

I pulled Chance up to the barn and swung off. "Guess that means I'm walking home," I said, mostly to myself.

"Usually, yes, but Mom told me to give you a ride home."

My eyes nearly popped out of my skull. I quickly tried to regain my composure. "By . . . horse?" I asked timidly, praying the answer would be yes. Let's just say Austin got his driver's permit, and he needed lots more practice. He chuckled at my comment.

"No." Seeing my shoulders slump slightly, he continued. "We aren't taking the truck either. Mom doesn't quite trust me on my own yet, even if it is just a short, dirt road trip to your place. We'll be taking the four-wheeler." I smiled. He was a slightly less crazy driver on the four-wheeler, so I shouldn't die.

"I wonder why she said that," I said, teasing him. It had always been like this, teasing and joking, sometimes friends, but more oftentimes enemies. He always thought he was the smarter one because he was slightly older than me. We wouldn't have gotten along at all except that Kat was my best friend.

Austin had reached the barn by now and retorted, "One day, you're going to be bleeding to death and there will be no one to help you get to the hospital but me, and I might just leave you there."

He was good at being snarky, but I was just as quick as him.

"Yeah, and when Kat found out, she would chunk you into the meat grinder."

His smile widened at that. "And I would be at peace with my decision," he said while placing a hand over his heart. Chance, Dash, and I approached the barn. Austin reached out to take Dash's lead rope from me and led the pony over to an empty stall. "Mom said it would be better to feed him by himself and then put him in with the others." He closed the door of the stall and turned toward me. "If you'll take Chance over to the corral, I'll get Calypso and Blitz out of their stalls."

Nodding, I clucked my tongue. "Come on, boy. Let's get you settled in for the night." Blowing out his nose in response, Chance followed me out behind the barn where the corral was. It was about the size of a rodeo arena, maybe a little smaller, plenty of space for four horses overnight.

Reaching the gate, I fiddled with the latch a little before it clicked open. I glanced over my shoulder as my ears heard a familiar whinny. Chance heard it too, flicking his ears up and spinning his head around. A happy noise of recognition escaped his lips. I led Chance through the gate and Austin, Blitz, and Calypso followed behind us. The black-and-white pinto picked up his pace into a prance, pulling against the lead rope Austin held. Chuckling, Austin unhooked his lead, allowing Blitz to roam free. I unclipped Chance's rope too, following Austin's example. He instantly met up with Blitz, who had entered the arena and started circling the perimeter, getting his bearings and instituting himself leader of the ring. Walking past me, Austin brought Calypso to a stop, petting her neck.

"Don't let 'em fool you," he whispered to her, just loud enough for me to hear. "You and I both know who the boss of this ring is." Releasing her, he began walking back over to me. "Dash should be done eating in a few minutes," he said. "We can bring him in after that. Mind helping me bring the feed for these horses from the barn?"

Nodding, I followed him past the gate and back to the beautiful, freshly painted, green barn. Reaching it, I could see a bag of premium horse feed and a wheelbarrow full of fresh hay beside it. Reaching the feed first, I hauled the bag up and over my shoulder.

"You want me to get that?" Austin asked, a hint of a smirk forming on his face. His parents had always raised him to be a gentleman, but I knew while he wasn't impolite to any of the girls at his school, he would never offer to help them with anything. The only reason he asked me was because it was something of a game between us. I knew he was no knight in shining armor saving the princess, and he knew I was no damsel in distress. I could handle myself.

"Why, good sir, that would be most helpful," I cooed dramatically. Snorting, I walked slightly ungracefully back to the corral, still carrying the bag of feed. Austin pushed the wheelbarrow directly behind me, intentionally hitting the back of my boots, trying to trip me. His charming attempts

50

to gracefully dispatch me came to an end as I reached the gate. Once inside the pen, I didn't bother shutting the gate behind me because one, Austin was right behind me, and two, when feed was involved, the horses kind of zoned out. They wouldn't try to escape. After feeding the horses, I went to fetch Dash, and Austin said he was off to get the four-wheeler.

I had just released Dash and exited the corral as he pulled up with a rumble. "I better hurry up and drop you off. It's already dark, and my dad still needs help with some of the livestock before the night is over." Without a word, I hopped on behind him. My arms instinctively hooked around his waist. Most girls I knew would pester me about how I was going on a "moonlit" ride home with a "cute boy." *No, just no.* I held on because I valued my life. Hit one pot hole, and the person in the back would be thrown off. Austin was a good driver most days. Others, well, no one lived to tell the tale. My parents trusted him, so did his parents. I, on the other hand, was still working on it.

We reached my house safely enough. He dropped me off with a nod of goodnight and zipped back to his house. I had a funny feeling in my stomach but decided it was due to all the excitement built up for camp tomorrow. I smiled goodnight to the sky and went inside for a restful sleep after a long day. I wished it could be that simple.

10

Rough Start

I WAS AWAKENED way before the alarm clock went off. When I first looked at the clock, I thought, *why are you up so early, body?* That was when my stomach clenched up, and I knew I had to get to the bathroom, *now*. My stomach decided it was a good time to start a revolt. So that was how my morning went. I got a stomachache that had me vomiting for an hour.

Normally, I was pretty good at tolerating pain, but when all the food I ate yesterday decided to make a reappearance, I didn't have much choice in the matter. My mom, being the wonderful lady she is, got up from her comfortable bed and began trying to nurse me back to health.

"Honey," she began softly. "I know you hate to hear this, but if you aren't better before church, you should probably stay in bed for the next day or two."

"I can't do that," I moaned. "The first day of camp is one of the most important. If I miss it, I could miss out on all of the best opportunities to look around before the camp gets packed." Mom had arranged for Kat, Austin, and me to get there the evening before the rest of the camp arrived. If I missed that, I wouldn't get the best bunk bed, and some were definitely better than others. From what I read online, there was also a limited number of sign-ups for some activities. *What if I missed out on all the best ones? What if Kat and I aren't doing the same activities?* Worst of all, I'd miss the one day where the camp was all empty and fresh, the rules hadn't been set yet, and I could explore.

"Let's see how you feel in a couple of hours, okay?" Mom proposed. "Take this medicine and try to go to sleep. If this is just food poisoning or something like that, I think you should be fine in a little bit. Don't worry about being late for camp. I'll come and check on you later."

She smiled reassuringly and closed the door softly behind her. After taking the medicine, I glanced at the clock. It read 5:49 a.m. I was so exhausted from the vomiting it didn't take long before I slumped into a dreamless sleep, hoping I wouldn't wake up until I felt better.

Sixteen . . . fifteen . . . fourteen minutes left. . . . My eyes kept straying to the luminescent green light of the clock in my mom's car. The numbers stubbornly took their sweet time in changing, which I guessed they could, since they *were* time. It wasn't fair I had to get sick the first day of Cowboy Camp. I was just happy I had gotten over it so quickly and was finally headed to camp. Kat, Austin, the horses, and all our tack had already been taken up there yesterday. Mom had seen how upset I was at not being able to get to camp the day before most people did. So, being the fantastic woman she was, offered to take me up there in the early morning hours before sunrise.

She didn't have to do that, but she did. If there was a mother-of-the-day award, she had everyone beat. Thirteen minutes now. Thirteen minutes until we would be at the Walden Creek Ranch where Cowboy Camp was held. I tried to focus on the mystery novel I was reading to pass the time, but I just couldn't. I probably read the same page eight times. Nine minutes left. I heard the radio fuzz back and forth between stations.

"The weather for the next few days is looking brighter by the minute—"

"Try our new shampoo. It's been proven better than any other name brand—"

"Call now and we'll double your order—a $40 value for just $19.99—"

The radio stations seemed to be out to bore people to death. I always wondered why all the stations seemed to play advertisements at the *exact* same time. Once you heard an advertisement come on, you couldn't find a station that was actually playing music. Four minutes. I let out a groan.

"How come the last few minutes of a trip feel the longest?" I asked. My mom just chuckled. She knew nothing she said would make me feel better, that is, except for the words—

"We're here." It took me a few moments to realize Mom had actually spoken. I jolted upright. Sure enough, my eyes were met with the most beautiful sight I had ever seen, well, almost the most beautiful.

11

Getting Settled

THERE WAS TOO much to see at once. The first thing my eyes focused on were the horses themselves: roans, duns, paints, sorrels, blacks, creams, and some patterns I didn't even recognize. They pranced and galloped in their enclosures, which were big enough for them to have some running distance, but too small for them to be in constantly. My face drew into a smile. That meant they wouldn't be there long—probably only at night. We would be riding them the rest of the time, a whole summer of almost constant riding.

I began to bounce up and down in my seat, acting half my age. The sun peeked over the horizon, painting the largest building that was dull red, a vibrant scarlet. Though it was clearly the oldest building on the premises, it stood tall and firm. The builders had obviously put a lot of time and effort into the construction. The cabins were sprinkled out on the left side of the large building. On the right side of "Big Red," as I dubbed the largest building, the five pens of horses resided. Slightly behind the horses, I saw a low-hanging, newly built, storehouse. Peering around Big Red, I saw an arena with bleachers on either side and a few other smaller empty practice pens farther off. In front and in between Big Red and the holding pens, I saw an open-air pavilion that would serve as the eating area. Two short and long buildings in the middle of the cabins looked like the bathrooms. All in all, this was my kind of camp. My mom pulled up next to Big Red, but before she could put the car in park, I had flung myself out into the beautiful morning.

"Finally," I yelled to no one in particular. To my right, I heard a joyous neigh. I saw Chance galloping in one of the smaller pens. He was accompanied by Calypso, Blitz, and three other horses I didn't recognize. Off to the side, I caught sight of Dash in a pen with a bunch of other cute ponies his size.

"It's about time." Redirecting my attention slightly to the left, I spied Austin coming out of the storage building, carrying a halter in one hand and a brush in the other. "Kat should be up soon," he called. Smiling, I remembered all the times I'd slept over at Kat's house. Austin had always been the early riser of the two. He claimed he didn't need as much beauty sleep as his sister, which always made me burst out in a fit of giggles. I couldn't help it.

All the girls I had ever met who had seen Austin said he was hot. But me, well, I knew him as my best friend's older brother. I had known him as long as I could remember. I wasn't a girl who looked at a guy and immediately thought *dang, that boy's attractive.* But I had to admit, Austin was pretty handsome. I would *not* be stupid enough to tell Kat though, or worse, Austin. I would never hear the end of it.

"Do you know where they put my stuff?" I asked him as I reached the gate he was about to enter to catch Blitz.

"Kat took it all to her cabin, number thirteen, I think," he answered.

"I only saw twelve," I responded, confused. He nodded over to a cabin on the outer edge of the camp, one I hadn't noticed before. It was older, that was for sure. Ivy grew up one side, and one of the three stairs was missing. Still, there was something magical about the place. "Thanks," I told Austin, turning back to him. But he had turned his attention to the horses.

Striding into the corral, he whistled. Several horses acknowledged his presence by twitching their ears toward his voice. One big, black-and-white pinto in particular came bounding over. Blitz threw his head up in the air with a jovial cry, happy to see his master. He was so excited to see him, in fact, that he almost barreled him over.

"Easy, boy," Austin grunted. "Remember you weigh *much* more than I do, you big klutz." Smiling, I left him to it.

It didn't take long for Mom to officially check me in at camp with one of the counselors. Then it was time for a goodbye hug. Mom passed me the few things I had brought and wished me luck. When her car disappeared around the bend, I sprinted to cabin thirteen, ready to see my best friend. I knew an adventure was about to begin.

Contrary to what Austin said, Kat was already up and had left the cabin before I arrived. I figured it was best to get myself situated first and then go find her.

Unpacking was easy. I didn't have too much stuff. Situating my tack in the store room was also easy. There were thirteen sections—divided according to cabin—and several slots in each section. I put my stuff in slot two in section thirteen. Lastly, I made sure Chance was still comfortable in the corral he had been put in last night. All of this went completely smoothly.

But then I met *them*. In the back of my head, I heard my mother's words. *God made everyone special. You have to get to know someone before you judge them. You can't judge someone instantly.*

Ha ha ha. Yes, I can, at least with these girls. Divas, was one way to describe them. They could also be described like every spoiled girls' club from a thousand different movies. They were just like the mean, popular girls from any movie you might watch. Okay, let me back up a few minutes.

"You there. Hey. I'm talking to you." I looked up and realized another teenager had been yelling at me. For a horrible minute, I thought it was Amy. The first thing I noticed was the way she dressed. She was wearing a hot pink sparkly V-neck top, skin-tight jeans, and heels so high they could have been classified as skyscrapers. She might have been pretty if she didn't have six or more layers of makeup on. Her jewelry was bright and flashy. The only thing that looked even the slightest bit soft was her hair. It came down to almost her waist in a golden waterfall that was only interrupted by a few strands of light pink. Behind her stood two other girls with their hands on their hips.

The girl on the left was a punk image of the first girl. Instead of all pink, she modeled her clothes in purple, dark green, and a small amount of black. Her hair was a pitch-black crown on top of her head. She would've been really intimidating if I hadn't had a recent growth spurt which left me two inches taller.

Rounding up the trio was a short girl of about five feet with pale skin and brown hair that turned blonde going down to her shoulders. I could never remember what that style was called. Her brown eyes were framed with glasses that made her look like she was smarter than people gave her credit for. If I had to guess, I would think she was the nicest of the three. As for her attire, she, like the other two, wore new name brand clothes. Unlike the others, she dressed with a little more modest taste.

The girl in pink brought me out of my thoughts with her constant talking and moaning. By the time I was focused on what she had been saying, she was halfway done, and all I'd caught was, "—and follow me to the cabins." I scrunched my eyebrows up in confusion, earning a groan from the teen. "I said come and help me take my bags to the cabin."

"Whoa whoa whoa," I started. "I am not a maid instructed to carry out your every whim."

"How much?" she asked.

"What?"

"How much to get you to carry our bags to cabin one?" she clarified, her tone indicating that I must be a dummy. My eyes got bigger every time she upped the price. She was up to $300 cash when I held up my hands.

"I'll carry your bags," I relented. "Just stop throwing around money you can't pay." When I said that, she just laughed like she knew something I didn't. *What turned you into the type of person who always thought you got everything you wanted? I'm not sure, but I am sure Amy and this girl would get along great. That or they'd be rivals.* Rolling my eyes mentally— because mother said I should never do it in front of the person because it was rude—I picked up the first bag and almost toppled over at the weight. Mustering my strength, I lugged the bag all the way across the camp and plopped it on the small porch of cabin one. Then I went and lugged the next one over, and the next one, and the next, and the next. Fifteen minutes later I dropped the last one off. Without any thanks, the pink girl, Jackie King as the bags labeled her, handed me a wad of cash. After a moment, I handed it back.

"I was just being neighborly," I said. "You don't need to pay me." Jackie shrugged and stuffed it back in her designer purse, turned around, and marched into their cabin. Mom had always taught me to be nice to people no matter what. If these girls didn't appreciate the work I did for them, then they weren't worth it.

Sighing, I turned around and went to find Kat. She was probably looking for a schedule so we would look like we were smart and knew what was going on, a task we sometimes failed at. Other students were moving in and out of the cabins, lugging suitcases and sleeping bags. Some of the kids drove themselves to camp, while others were dropped off by a parent like I was.

I decided to look in the main office first, where check-ins were taking place. It was a little room attached to the inside left corner of Big Red that looked kind of odd and out of place like it had been added on more recently. I found the door open and strolled in.

The shelves lining the wall were stuffed to the brim with folders, papers, and lots and lots of nick-knacks, making the place look like a hurricane had a party. A quick scan of the room revealed that Kat wasn't here, just the two counselors handling check-ins and a few students and parents. As I left the cramped room, I had an idea. It was just after breakfast. She had probably gone to find something to eat. My stomach growled in agreement. Breakfast was a good idea.

I found Kat sitting in the pavilion munching on some French toast and eggs. She looked up just as she was finishing her eggs, and her eyes got big the instant she saw me. Her eyes always did that when she was overly excited about something. As I came closer, I realized it had to be the beginning of an adventure, because she jumped up from her spot and charged toward me, a grin spread from ear to ear.

12

Rules And Regulations

THERE WAS A meeting for all the campers that evening. Today had been a day of settling in and getting the horses comfortable in their new surroundings. Tomorrow, camp activities would officially start. Kat and I had arrived at Big Red early to get a good place to sit. About fifty metal folding chairs had been set up facing the far side where a small platform stood. So far, the kids I had seen today were anywhere from nine years old to eighteen. I didn't know anyone but Austin and Kat. My cousin Riley had been a senior last year, so she wouldn't be here. I wasn't too worried about meeting new people though.

Kat had heard from her dad that those who were under thirteen would stay for two weeks, instead of two months. The rest, who stayed all summer, got to participate in the Horsemanship Olympics, as was tradition here. I was bubbling with excitement over the Olympics. Kat was too, but out of the two of us, I was by far the most competitive. If there was one person more competitive than me, it was Austin. Austin and Blitz would be a force to be reckoned with for sure.

I was just thinking this when a man took the stage. Anyone who saw this man would instantly recognize him for what he was: a cowboy to the core. He wore what any man who lived on a ranch would wear: a pair of old blue jeans, well-worn boots, a work shirt, belt, and of course, his Stetson.

But he didn't just look the part. He carried himself like a true westerner. He didn't need to quiet anyone, because from the moment he stepped onstage, the crowd went silent. Everyone probably felt the same thing. They knew this guy was the boss. If he was like most cowboys, he would rarely put up with a lot of crazy kids. It was best to act respectful or suffer the consequences.

If he was like my dad and you made him mad, you would spend the rest of the day doing chores with no point to them. Readjusting the firewood stack in the middle of summer when you wouldn't need a fire for *months* was one of my dad's personal favorites. I didn't get the last splinter out of my hand until September.

"I hope everyone came well rested," he started. "If you came to this camp to relax in a pool all day, then you're sure to be disappointed. For those of you who came for a chance to improve your horsemanship skills and bond with your horse along the way, good. The next few days are going to be long, full of heat, sweat, and hopefully, fun." He paused for a moment, gauging the audience.

"I'm Wyatt, the guy in charge here," the man continued. "If you attended Cowboy Camp last year, then I'm glad you're back. However, last year we had a few kids who didn't think it was their duty to do the things I asked them, mainly following the rules. I'm starting off this year a little differently. I'm telling y'all this now so you have no excuses later." He paused again, and I rethought my statement about cowboys earlier. Some cowboys could talk more than just a few sentences at a time. He had started speaking again, so I focused my attention back on him.

"This is my land we're standing on," Wyatt said. "That means you follow my rules."

A couple of the kids nodded or mumbled a "*yes, sir.*"

"I'm going to go through these rules as fast as I can so we aren't here all night. So, listen up." He held up a finger. "Number one. There will be no boys in the girl cabins, and no girls in the boy cabins. Girls have the odd numbered cabins, and guys stay in the evens." He held up another finger. "Number two. Breakfast is at 7:30. If you stayed up until three a.m. the night before, that's not my fault. Get yourself down to breakfast." He finished by rattling off the rest of the rules. He then had two of the younger boys pass out sheets of paper with the rules on them. "For those of you forgetful people," he said, emphasizing that some people were intentionally forgetful. "You will have no excuse, so behave."

When the paper came to me, I examined it.

<u>How to not get kicked out of Cowboy Camp</u>
Seriously, follow these rules.

1. No guys in the girl cabins or girls in the guy cabins.

2. Get yourself to all meals, especially breakfast. I don't care if you're exhausted from staying up all night, that's your fault.

3. The woods are off-limits unless you get permission from one of the camp leaders.

4. Attend all the activities you are assigned to. Don't make us come looking for you.

5. If you damage <u>anything,</u> you will be expected to pay for it.

6. No fooling around near the horses.

7. If you go through a gate that is closed, make sure it is closed when you leave it. If a gate is open, leave it that way.

8. Obey everything your camp leaders tell you.

9. Use common sense. Don't do something stupid.

Pretty straight forward, I thought. That was how I liked it. He went on to list a few announcements such as what time

67

the morning activities were and where they would be held. I was listening carefully for most of it, but as he went on, I got a little sidetracked. I focused back on what he was saying the moment I heard, "—teammates for the Horsemanship Olympics. While only the campers staying full time will be scored at the end of the summer, all the campers will get a partner for the remainder of their stay for teamwork building exercises and some other activities."

I immediately was mentally injected with eight cups of sugar. *Teammates? That would be amazing. I could be on a team with Kat. We would be unstoppable.* I slapped myself mentally. There would be many other teams competing, a lot of them were probably talented kids. I was sure Austin was going to be trouble. This was not going to be an easy win. But with Kat, Chance, and Calypso, we would surely pack a punch. At least, if my ego didn't get in the way, as my mom always told me.

"I hope I get put on a team with someone I know," Kat whisper-shouted in my ear.

"What?" I whisper-shouted back at her, confused. I turned my head toward her as she explained herself.

"Weren't you listening? He said we wouldn't be picking our partner," her voice was rushed, but quiet. "We would be assigned one by the staff, and there would be no changing it. He wants us to meet new people. He explained it would also be a test of skills to see if we would be able to work with anyone we were partnered with."

I'm pretty sure I stopped breathing for a second. My palms began to sweat. *This is bad, really bad. Depending on who my partner is, I could place last before we even start.* I tried to remember what I had learned a few weeks ago in Sunday school. *It's in the book of Galatians, but what chapter? Oh, Galatians 6:4. But each person should examine his own work, and then he will have a reason for boasting in himself alone, and not in respect to someone else.* I took a deep breath. I would be fine. No matter who I was paired up with, I would work with them and be nice. Even if it meant that we placed dead last.

13

Teammates

IT WAS EARLY on the third day of Cowboy Camp. The days had been packed with nonstop activities, games, and learning. Mornings were dedicated to roping and herding cattle lessons. The counselors made games out of it to test our skills. Whether you had to race another team to rope the calf or section off the numbered calves to their designated stalls in the fastest time, the camp instructors would always teach us something and test us to keep us on our toes. I thrived under the pressure, the challenge. Euphoria rushed through me whenever I successfully demonstrated I had learned what they were teaching us.

After lunch, we had an hour of free time followed by lessons in barrel racing, pole weaving, and many other games. There were water games too. One day was canoeing, and another day water balloon fights broke out everywhere. Dinner was always a big affair because all the kids had worked up quite an appetite throughout the day. In the evening, we all gathered around the campfire at the end of the pavilion and sang silly campfire songs, chatted with friends over what had happened that day, and got all the latest, juiciest gossip. *We've only been here a couple of days. How do they already have gossip?* Kat and I were usually tired out by then, so we hit the hay right after, but we were up early the next day, brushing and grooming our sleepy horses.

Mom always said I was a weird child. That was fine with me, it meant I didn't share most people's taste in some things. Which also meant that Kat and I had our own cabin all to ourselves. No one else seemed to want to stay in the "old and haunted" cabin.

Needless to say, the first few days of camp had been a blast, and there hadn't been a single bump in the road until the teammate list went up that morning.

My resolve to work with whomever I got put with evaporated as soon as I saw the list. I would've been good with someone I barely knew. I would've even been okay with a stranger. But the person I got paired with was the last person on earth I would have chosen for my partner. *Okay, maybe I'm exaggerating. Actually, no I'm not.*

The name Hope Watkins sat in bold right next to the one and only Jackie King. My heart plummeted to my shoes. *I had to work with her? No. This is impossible. There must be a mistake.*

71

I tried to rein in my disappointment. Surely Kat would get paired up with someone good. If I couldn't win, I at least wanted her to have a fighting chance at the championship. But as I looked at the list a second time to find out who she was paired with, I realized we had both gotten the short end of the stick. Her partner wasn't nearly as bad as mine, but it was still a low blow. She was paired with Tiffany Stratton. I recognized her as the third girl of The Diva Posse, as the camp had begun to call them. From the little I knew about her, she was indeed the nicest of the three girls, but she would still be a pain to work with.

I took a deep breath. *Be optimistic, Hope. You can find a way to make this work. You have to.*

14

Finding Common Ground

OPTIMISM WASN'T GOING to help with Jackie. I had been trying all day to find something we both loved or at least something we both agreed on. From what I could tell, it was more likely I would grow wings. We didn't like the same movies. We didn't have the same passion for music. She was boy crazy, and I was not. We both rode horses, but for *totally* different reasons. She liked how she looked on a horse, but she treated her horse like a machine. The mare was there to do her bidding and make her look good. *Ugh.* I severely disliked people who treated horses like that. At least Amy had been fascinated with horses, wanting to learn everything she could about them.

The only reason I didn't load up Jackie's mare then and there was because I learned she had someone else taking care of her horse's day-to-day needs back home. The horse basically had her own butler. It was a small consolation. Plus, her horse was spoiled rotten with the best of everything: feed, tack, grooming, and stalls. She could've been a lot worse off.

There was one other thing we both liked, *Austin*. But also, for *completely* different reasons. I thought of Austin as my best friend's brother, the guy I could count on if everyone else happened to be busy. He was an amigo, buddy, pal, chum of chums. To me, he was just Austin. To Jackie, he was "a good boy who needed to be shown a good time" and "the hottest boy on the planet #FutureBoyfriend." So, to say we had different passions would be an understatement. I was doing my best to work with her, but my best might not be enough.

"How much longer are you going to work at it? You're hopeless. Your arm looks like an overcooked noodle. You missed again. And again." I stifled a moan. Jackie had kept up a running commentary of everything I did wrong. I was working on my roping skills. Jackie was supposed to be working on her technique as well, but that would've meant quitting giving me "advice." Since I didn't do well in the calf roping sessions we had been having at camp, I knew I was going to need a lot of practice.

One of our camp leaders, Jamie Lancaster, had suggested I practice with Jackie to help us get to know each other. In less than fifteen minutes, I had learned enough about her to know that I severely disliked—Mom didn't like the word hate—Jackie. She loved to shop, talk about boys, and tell others how to do something she didn't even know how to do. She was really getting on my nerves.

I tried to focus on the roping dummy I was working on. I raised the rope above my head again and began twirling it, faster and faster and faster. When I was ready, I released the lasso, and it sailed through the air, actually flying toward the plastic calf this time. As it hit the calf and I tightened the rope, it snapped loose and flew back to me. *Well, I stink.* I looked up at the sound of giggling.

Two little nine-year-old girls had been watching me through the bars of the practice ring and had seen me epically miss. I had seen these two girls around before. One had dark skin and straight black hair that fell to her shoulders and into her eyes. I think her name was Zoe, and the other I remembered was Chloe. She had bright red hair that was naturally wild and curly. Her skin was pink on part of her face and arms. She loved to be outdoors every waking hour, so she sun-screened by the can. I could relate. I had pretty fair skin too when I was younger. Over the years though, my skin had tanned a little and was more used to the sun's relentless attacks. The little girls kind of reminded me of myself at their age, and they were as cute as their names.

"You're not very good at that," Chloe choked out through her giggling. Zoe elbowed her in the gut and gave her a disapproving look. I cracked a smile at them.

"No, I'm not very good, am I?" I said. "That's why I've got to practice."

Jackie groaned again behind me where she sat on the edge of the fence.

"You know, practicing when you're that bad is pointless," she told me. I refused to give in to her resigned attitude. I wasn't going to throw in the towel just like that. I turned back to the roping dummy, and the little girls roamed off. Jackie pulled out her phone and got on Snapchat or some other pointless social media app. I could tell because she held the phone out at arm's length and did her best impression of a duck. She must've taken that same picture from a million different angles of the practice ring. When I turned back toward her after another twenty minutes or so of practice, she was still posing in front of the camera. *How does her phone battery last after a whole day of that?*

"You want to try a time or two?" I asked her. I wanted to make it sound like I was asking her opinion. I didn't want to sound bossy, but roping was one of the things they would judge us on at the Horsemanship Olympics. I knew I would probably only be average, even with all the practice I was putting in, which meant Jackie's extra effort would be essential to keeping up with the other teams.

"Why would I want to spend my time throwing a rope around all day?" she questioned. The tone in her voice made it seem like she was talking to a toddler who wanted to play in the trash can.

"Because it's a valuable life lesson in these parts." She arched her right eyebrow, telling me she didn't agree with my reasoning. "And it's part of the games, and we get points for it. It'll help us win," I said, switching tactics. "You do like to win, don't you?"

"Of course." A new gleam filled her eyes. She jumped off the fence and closed the space between us in just a few steps. "Give me that," she told me sharply, reaching out and taking the lasso from my grasp. It looked like we now had three things in common.

I would be lying if I said she was good. Truth was, she was *really* good. I stood there with my mouth hanging open in amazement as she twirled, threw, and caught. Out of the fifteen attempts she made, she only missed three times. She tried from all different angles like she was taking pictures or like a basketball player played Around the World. After sending the lasso one more time around the calf, she turned back to me. I just had time to snap my mouth shut before she saw me gawking. Her stance of superiority helped me to be less awestruck. I composed myself and said as calmly and evenly as I could, "Since it's clear you're the better of the two of us, would you mind showing me how you did that?" I hoped the flattery would soften her up.

"Maybe another time," she answered. "I need to go find Harley and Tiffany. I think I'll faint if I don't get any food soon." She strutted off after announcing this and dropped the lasso in the dirt, not giving me a second glance. I would bet money she had said that so she wouldn't have to teach me. She probably loved being better at something than someone else. I only hoped she didn't love it so much she would sacrifice any chance of placing in the competition we had.

15

Phone Service

IT HAD BEEN a few days since the roping incident. Jackie had given me excuse after excuse after excuse, and I was tired of it. But there wasn't anything I could do. Still, I had been getting a little better. I listened as carefully as possible in the big group lessons the camp leaders directed. I practiced a lot by trial and error. I wished I could practice with Kat, but the camp leaders told us they wanted us to practice with our teammates and form bonds with them. I tried a few times to explain to Jamie Lancaster the situation my "teammate" was putting me in, but she assured me Jackie would come around eventually. I didn't believe her. Needless to say, my improvement rate was excruciatingly slow. Finally, I had enough of Jackie's nonsense. I was going to find her and get her to work with me, even if one of us died in the process.

I searched in the barn. Nothing. I searched the pastures the horses were in. Still, I found nothing. She wasn't at the dining pavilion, and I checked every cabin. I knocked on the boys' cabins and just barged into the girls' cabins. No one knew where she was. My final attempt to find her was to check the main office. She wasn't there either, but Mr. Wyatt was.

"Do you know where I can find Jackie King?" I inquired. He looked up from his desk and crossed his arms over the papers scattering the desk, then interlocked his fingers.

"I'm not quite sure. Have you checked her cabin?"

"Yes."

"The pavilion?"

"I've checked *everywhere,* sir." I emphasized the word everywhere, because I *had* checked thoroughly. She was obviously avoiding me.

"Well, I'm sure she's around somewhere. You probably missed her." He paused. "Though, she could be trying to find a signal."

"Signal?" I asked.

"The only phone that works way out here is this one." He indicated an eggshell-colored phone hanging on the wall. Above it hung a list of all the emergency numbers and other important frequent callers. "She came in so often to use it I had to ban her," he chuckled. "She didn't like that too much."

"Oh." I understood a little more now. Jackie was the kind of girl to freak out without cell service. "I guess I didn't notice since I don't have a cell phone."

"You don't seem like the girl who would notice even if she did," he countered. *Touché.*

"What are the papers for?" I asked.

He looked at me carefully, like he was trying to figure out how much to tell me. "Plans for an activity we'll have later in the summer," he replied simply. I sensed from the way he said it this was as much information as I was going to get.

"Okay, well, if you see Jackie, can you tell her the teammate she is avoiding is looking for her?"

He nodded, and I left the office, wondering about the papers and what the secret activities were. I wasn't paying much attention to where I was going. I was lost in thought. My feet seemed to direct themselves as they covered the well-trodden ground at a swift pace. *Why do they need to keep the activities a secret? Will there be a final test for all of us, or better yet, a showdown for the best of us? That would be so cool.* I was continuing down this train of thought when I was interrupted by a sudden cracking sound. I looked up, startled.

The scenery had changed. A cool breeze ruffled the loose, flyaway hairs that had escaped my ponytail. The sun no longer burned my face. I looked up at the colossal tree branches overhead. My ears overloaded on all the different sounds of wildlife I hadn't been able to hear at the main buildings. Birds, small creatures, a babbling brook not too far away, and many other secrets were bound to be hidden from my view. I caught a quick glance of a rabbit bounding swiftly out of sight behind a bush. *This place is beautiful.* I breathed in deeply, reveling in the sweet smell of these woods. *These woods. Uh oh. Why am I in the woods? That's against the rules. I could get sent home.* I swung around and began making my way swiftly back toward the corrals, which was the closest landmark I was allowed to be at. I came to an abrupt halt when I heard someone give an angry outburst.

"Curse you. Why won't you work?" I spun around, trying to locate the speaker. Bright pink stood out so easily against the background of trees I was surprised I missed the figure earlier. The girl spotted me and glared. "What are you staring at?" I came to my senses at her accusatory tone.

"Nothing. How long have you been here? I've been looking for you all afternoon."

"It's none of your business, but I'm trying to get at least one bar in this barren wasteland. I have important calls that need to be made."

"Important calls?" I asked skeptically. "I'm sure whoever you are trying to contact can live without you for a while longer. If it's really important, they can call the main office phone." I tried to say all of this without sounding exasperated, but Jackie was really getting on my nerves. I was trying my best to figure out how she was unique, give her the benefit of the doubt. She was making it extremely difficult. To my surprise, Jackie put her phone in her pocket and sauntered over to me.

"I suppose they will have to survive. Did you come to pester me yet again about roping lessons?"

"Yes, well, I'm not meaning to pester you," I said. "I just really need some help and you're the only one who is allowed to tutor me besides the counselors, and they're all too busy." At this point, I was doing my best to be polite. I was also doing my best to appeal to her human side.

She seemed to take the bait this time because she looked at me in pity. "I guess I should help you. Otherwise, you'll make us the laughingstock of the entire camp. And there are too many cute boys here. I can't let them think we are both incompetent."

Of course, she is worried about what the boys think. I gritted my teeth, determined to take her insults. I had to.

I forced myself to think about something else, like getting out of these woods without getting caught. We made our way out of the trees as quickly as possible.

16

Competitive Newbie

"TURN HIM TIGHTER, Danny. Faster now. That's the way." Our barrel racing instructor, Mrs. Karen, shouted commands, and Danny Taylor followed them with practiced ease. Two days after the incident in the woods, I had mostly forgotten about my accidental trip. It was easy, considering we had started practicing on one of my favorite events: barrel racing. Right now, we were watching Danny, an eighteen-year-old avid barrel racer, show us how it was done. Danny rode a twelve-year-old bay quarter horse named Staccato. The gelding had earned his name, I could tell. These were no beginners. Whoever had gotten Danny as a teammate would have a serious leg up in this part of the competition. I tried to focus on the pair as much as possible. I needed to be better at barrel racing than I was at roping.

Though I had been practicing hard and Jackie had dubbed me "adequate," there was still much to be desired. I would have to continue to work on my roping at the same time as I was working on learning new skills like barrel racing. I knew I would love doing it because I loved watching at rodeos, and I loved racing with Kat. But I had never actually barrel raced before. Sure, I had set up barrels at my house a few times, but they had never been accurately set up. The barrels needed to be set exactly the right distance apart from each other, the ring had to be big enough, and the ground had to be worked over so it was smooth and the rider didn't have to worry about looking for holes. All of this had to be just right, or the rider and horse couldn't go at top speed, at least, not safely.

All of this rushed through my head as I watched Danny and Staccato swing around the last barrel and come tearing back toward the entry gate. Once they were through, everyone surrounding the ring burst out into applause. Mrs. Karen continued what she had been saying, instructing us on the basic principles of barrel racing. She taught us what to do and what to veer away from doing. By the time she was done, my brain felt like the turkey on Thanksgiving, stuffed and dead. She had us each go around the barrels, once walking, once trotting, and once at a lope. Walking was easy, so was trotting. Chance had been pretty easygoing today. He was a smart horse and figured out the pattern quickly.

It was soon my turn again, and this time, I got to lope. Chance quivered beneath me, as if he knew he got to run. "Easy, boy, here we go," I murmured to him. Our instructor gave us a nod, signaling we were free to go. I released the tension in Chance's reins and kicked him lightly with my heels. That little motion was all he needed as encouragement. He lunged forward at a full gallop, breaking away for the first barrel. He was a little too excited for my liking. I clamped my teeth shut to keep from biting my tongue off. My arms were stiff as I pulled back slightly on the reins.

"Calm down, boy," I got out through gritted teeth. He slowed down only slightly and swung around the first barrel. His turn was wide and far away from the barrel. I continued to apply pressure to the reins until he slowed to a lope. We came around the second barrel closer and bumped it. It almost fell over but didn't. The last barrel was the smoothest turn, but as soon as Chance cleared it, he bolted. His stride lengthened, and his neck stretched to its full length. Dad would say "his mustang was showing." I hadn't seen a stable-bred horse who was as fast as Chance yet. He reminded me of this whenever I forgot, like now. We passed the entry gates, and it was only then that Chance began to slow down. I circled him back around to the outside of the ring. *That was terrifying but so much fun.*

As we came up to the group, I could see Mrs. Karen was frowning at me. I thought I saw something like a glint of amusement flicker through her eyes briefly, but then, it was gone.

"In the future, keep your horse at a lope. I won't have inexperienced kids breaking their necks because they're showing off." Mrs. Karen's voice was colder than usual. I nodded to acknowledge I had heard her. She was angry, that much was obvious. But there was something in her eyes I couldn't quite read. "Not bad for a newbie," she muttered. I probably wasn't supposed to hear that, so I kept a straight face.

"Alright, guys, that's enough for today. Keep working on it. Please do not go any faster than a lope in your practices unless a chaperon thinks you're ready enough to try faster and is watching you." She looked at all of us in turn, studying our faces to make sure we were paying attention to what she had been saying. A few times, she gave the stink eye to some of the younger, rowdier, boys.

When she got to Danny, Mrs. Karen said, "All of those rules apply to you too, Danny. I won't be showing any favoritism today." Danny laughed and pretended to be offended. Her face contorted into one of shock and then morphed into her usually goofy smile. She didn't need much practice, and she knew it. Everybody knew it. I figured we were all thinking the same thing. *I'm keeping my eye on Danny. She's a nice girl, but she's serious competition.*

17

Practicing

THE NEXT DAY, Jackie and I were scheduled to share the arena with Kat and her teammate. *What is her name again?* Kat had told me before, I just always forgot. *Tamie? Taffy? Tiffany? Yes, Tiffany Stratton, the more modest and not-such-a-pain of The Diva Posse.* At least, from what Kat told me. I may have been partnered with someone I didn't like much, but even that couldn't dull my mood today. It was the first day Kat and I actually got to practice together, the first day to spend some quality time together in a while.

Sure, we had seen each other at mealtimes and in the mornings and evenings, but it wasn't enough. I hadn't even gotten to see much of her during free time because I had been working so hard on my roping. But today was different, and I was determined to make it count.

"So, how does it feel to be on the lousiest team on the ranch?" I looked over to see Kat with a smile on her lips that said she was trying hard not to burst into a fit of giggles.

"I don't know," I whispered back. "Never had the feeling before. Shouldn't I be asking you?"

Kat let her mouth drop in a comical impression of someone who was shown a bowl full of macaroni covered in guacamole. Jackie was going around the barrels and Tiffany was immensely focused on her, so they didn't hear our conversation.

"Tiffany isn't actually all that bad," Kat begrudgingly admitted. "It's more like she goes with whatever her group does. When we're alone, she acts like a regular human being. It's only when Jackie or Harley are with her that she's bad."

"Harley's the punk, right? The second-in-command of their posse?" I asked.

"Yeah. She's paired up with a girl from Texas, I think," Kat confirmed. "So, is Jackie really a terrible person, or is she just a preprogrammed robot?"

"Now that you mention the robot, not a bad guess," I said. "I can't come up with anything better for a backstory. Jackie won't talk a lot when it's just us. She only speaks when she needs to tell me my outfit stinks or that I'm doing something terribly wrong. I don't know a whole bunch about her, except of course, that someone in her family must be filthy rich, the way she throws money around."

"You really don't know anything else about her?"

"Well, she's good at roping. She's been teaching me."

"Ouch." Kat winced in sympathy. "She's not as bad as Amy, is she?"

"It'd be an interesting matchup," I commented. "But Jackie does have her moments. She's honest, at least. Just a pain to deal with." I thought of the patience she had showed once she actually decided she wanted to work with me, her calm and collectedness when she told me what I needed to change. "Most of what she says may be mean or to the point, but during our practices where she's actually working, she hasn't once yelled at me. That's got to be something."

"I bet you she's competitive." Kat thought a bit more and continued. "She doesn't want a partner who is going to pull her down. Remember, all the points are a combined score for each of the players on a team."

"Hey," I yelled, realizing what she just said. "I'm not going to drag her down."

Kat looked at me sheepishly. "You're a good horsewoman. You're great on Chance and a fast learner. But with roping, well . . ." She trailed off, waiting for me to finish her sentence.

"I stink," I finally admitted. I shifted my gaze to watch Tiffany come around the last barrel and lope back home. From what I saw, it was a clean run. Chance quivered and shifted beneath me. He'd been sitting in one place too long, and he wanted to get moving. So did I. I needed to get this under my belt faster than roping. I needed to redeem myself.

"I'm going to make up for my roping by being fantastic at barrel racing," I said. "You should see Chance swing around the barrels. He's a natural." If ever I needed proof that Chance could understand human speech, I would have it. He puffed himself out to look bigger. His neck arched in a macho way. He always had a way of making me look good.

"I'd like to see it," Kat said, grinning. She had noticed Chance's stallion-ish behavior. Calypso on the other hand, looked unimpressed. I clucked to Chance and spun him around toward the gate marking the starting line. Once there, I got him facing the barrels and looked over to my right at the counselor watching our progress today. She nodded, telling me I was good to go.

I took a breath and kicked Chance. He made a jolting movement forward, almost jumping into the air. He'd been doing this since the first time. I was not allowed to let him go faster than a lope, but he apparently didn't understand the human word "slower" or he pretended to forget. He tried to race toward the first barrel on the right. I kept a steady pull on his reins to keep him from breaking the "no faster than a lope" rule. He didn't seem to feel it much, or it didn't compare to his yearning to run, or better yet, fly. In seconds, it felt like, we passed the first barrel and were quickly closing in on the second. Chance had basically figured out himself how to swing around the barrels. I needed to keep myself centered and balanced, but he did most of the rest. Maybe it was his inborn mustang.

The agility of the mustangs had to be high to keep them moving. Their legs were their most powerful tools, especially in the open range. Mustangs needed to be faster than everything else they came upon, and that included making sharp turns without falling over or hitting something.

We were circling the last barrel now, and my arms were throbbing from exertion. Instead of my arms getting used to the stain of holding Chance back, they hurt worse each time. It seemed like everything in Chance and me wanted to do anything but go slower. We came to the gate and slowed to a trot. Chance pranced around, only rejuvenated by our lap around the barrels.

"Hope Watkins," a stern voice called out. I maneuvered Chance to face the direction the voice had come from. Mrs. Karen was standing beside the counselor who had been watching us practice. She was wearing the usual for everyone around here: jeans, a thin button-up shirt with a camisole underneath, a hat, and boots. She had her hands clasped together and propped up on the fence, staring back at me with a look of curiosity. I couldn't tell if it was a generally mad curiosity or something else.

"You ever barrel raced before?" she asked. By the tone of her voice, I could tell she didn't like something I'd been doing.

"Not until here," I replied. I pulled Chance up beside the bars the counselor and Mrs. Karen were leaning up against on the other side of the fence.

"That's not barrel racing," Mrs. Karen corrected. "Barrel racing is flying at breakneck speed across a course of three barrels. You've been play acting." I tried to interrupt, to tell her I was going as fast as she'd allowed me to, but she kept talking before I could say anything. "That mustang of yours has more power than most horses can muster, and I won't have it squandered. Next time you go around the barrels, I want you actually doing it."

"You mean—"

"I want you to let him *fly*."

I stared at her, stunned. She hadn't even let Danny, a girl who'd been barrel racing for years, run the barrels at full speed since the demonstration. I kept my mouth shut when she was about to say something else, probably that I shouldn't, in fact, let Chance run. But she didn't say anything. I kicked Chance around and walked him briskly to the imaginary starting line. He was buzzing beneath me now. He obviously understood the human word "racing."

Chance swung around to face the barrels automatically, positioned directing in line with the third and final barrel on the opposite end of the arena. My breathing had already begun to grow shallow. Chance was a mess beneath me. He had been begging for this for the longest time, and now I got to let him run. I glanced over at the women leaning against the fence. Mrs. Karen nodded.

Chance made his jumping jolt again, but this time it wasn't as bad. It was more exhilarating. I didn't have to pull him back. Just like the first time around the barrels, his neck lowered, his legs lengthened, and his mane and tail were streaming behind us in billowing black smoke trails. The first barrel came up on us twice as fast as I was used to, and I struggled to get myself centered when he spun around it. He almost tripped because of his off-balanced companion but shifted his weight to catch me and zipped to the next barrel like nothing happened. I was more ready for the next one. I pulled back on the reins to slow him down ever so slightly on the turn, and I made sure to balance correctly this time. As soon as he cleared the barrel, I let him run as fast as he wanted toward the final barrel. It was our cleanest turn this lap, and as Chance carried us home, I was sure this was how it felt to fly.

It took a few moments for the adrenaline rush to ease up and the sound of clapping to reach my ears. Kat, Jackie, Tiffany, the counselor, and even Danny—I had no idea when she showed up—were all clapping enthusiastically. Mrs. Karen had a smile on her face.

"I didn't know I had competition," Danny yelled after me. The way she said it wasn't mean, like she thought she was the only good one; it was surprise and excitement for a contender. "Seriously, you've all been holding out on me." Danny had a big grin on her face. Her happiness for another fellow rider, even if it was for another team, wasn't easily missed. She was a great sport, and that was hard to come by.

I just hoped they didn't all see something in me that could just be luck.

"Not flight yet, but he shows potential. That first turn left some things to be desired," Mrs. Karen commented from a couple of feet away. "But your horse has a good sense of where your balance needed to be. He caught your weight this time. You noticed your mistake and fixed it the next turn. Let's just make sure it doesn't happen again, though. The horse is doing the harder job. Let's not make it harder."

Mrs. Karen had reached the end of the ring where I stood by this time and stretched a hand out to stroke Chance. "He's a fast and intelligent horse," she said softly, almost inaudibly. She added more loudly, "Walk him around the ring three more times and then put him up. Don't let him run the barrels. I want him to take off like he just did every time. When a horse wants to race, don't let him have too much of it. I like that fire, and I don't want him to lose it." She finished her instructions with two pats on his neck and then strolled away to work with some other students who were entering the ring to warm up for their turn around the barrels.

"That was awesome," Kat said and held her hand up for a high five.

I obliged.

"It almost makes everyone forget what a bad roper you are," she continued.

Leave it to Kat to be the one to keep me grounded. I laughed at her crazy grin. She was the best friend I could ever have, really.

She was close enough to me to tell me straight to my face what was up. "I'm going to go around the barrels now," she said. "Whatever happens, you need to cheer like I just won a million dollars for being the fastest barrel racer in the world." She held a hand beside her mouth. "Calypso's nervous until she hears someone cheering her name." Kat winked at me, like we were sharing a secret and Calypso was on the other side of the ring, not right below us.

When Kat gently kicked Calypso to get her to move, she trotted slowly to the starting place. Calypso's entire body was different from Chance's. His nerves came from excitement. She was just straight up nervous. Kat kicked her into motion, and she moved at a graceful—if slightly jittery—lope. Their lap around the barrels was smooth enough and actually quite good for beginners. Like me, Kat was a novice in barrel racing. But the way I cheered, nobody would ever have thought that.

18

Announcement

I WAS WALKING to the pavilion for lunch when I noticed there were more kids gathered than usual. Usually, only half a dozen or so kids ate at a time in the pavilion. Today though, it seemed almost all of them were here, minus of course, the nine through twelve-year-old kids who had gone home after their two-week camp. I spotted Kat and Austin walking a few feet ahead of me with another guy. I jogged to catch up.

"Anyone know what's up with all the kids converging?" I asked when I reached them.

"Maybe steak is on the menu for today's lunch," The boy walking beside Austin answered. "Or maybe even tacos," he joked. His smile was wide, showing his white teeth that were only sharpened by the warm hue of his skin. "My name's

Zeke, by the way." He reached out his hand and I shook it. He seemed like a pretty easygoing guy. I bet Austin and him were good friends.

"He's my teammate," Austin told me, as if he'd read my mind. "And for your information, we're an amazing duo. You and Kat better watch out." *Of course, Austin would get competitive.* Considering that all three of us were super competitive when it came to anything we did, it was a miracle we hadn't gotten ourselves killed, or more likely, killed one of the others.

"I will watch out for who is going to be placed right behind my team, in second." Before Austin or Kat had time to respond with a snarky comment, we reached the pavilion and the crowd.

They were gathered around a large beam that the announcements were attached to. Most of the pages hadn't changed since the beginning of Cowboy Camp: team schedules, cabin inspections, and training sessions with the camp instructors along with some other stuff. But a new page had been added since the last time I checked it yesterday. Today there was a page that read *"Big meeting at one o'clock today in the dining pavilion. All campers are required to be there."* It said nothing else.

"Sounds like we're in trouble," Kat said to my right.

"Which means no tacos or steak," Zeke agreed glumly. I would've chuckled, but then I realized Zeke had put the notion of steak in my head, and I too, was very disappointed. I looked at the paper again. *I hope we're not in trouble.*

"Maybe it's something to do with the competition at the end of Cowboy Camp," Austin speculated. "If someone did something bad and is getting in trouble for it, they wouldn't have asked everyone to come." What Austin said made sense, and for some reason, what he said made me think of something else. I hadn't thought about it since it happened, but Mr. Wyatt had been pretty suspicious when I had gone to the main office to look for Jackie the day she went missing. Those papers he had been looking at—*plans for something later this summer. Was this those plans being realized?* I glanced at my watch. We had thirty minutes before we found out.

Thirty minutes was a long time to wait for something, at least, if that something could be anything. Kat and I had eaten lunch by now and were just eavesdropping, or causally happening to hear, in on conversations happening around us. Austin and Zeke were sitting with some other guys at a different table, laughing at a joke someone must have just told. They looked like they were having a blast. I on the other hand, was breaking out in hives from stress. My least favorite activity? Knowing something was coming and waiting for it but not knowing what that *it* was.

I drummed my fingers on the table in a therapeutically soothing manner. I glanced at my watch for the tenth time in the past thirty minutes. But this time was not like the others. This time, it actually said the meeting should be starting. As soon as I thought this, Mrs. Karen called for our attention from the front of the pavilion, near the table with all the food.

"Everyone, quiet down," she yelled to be heard over the campers' cacophony of noise. It took another yell before everyone quieted down. "As you all know," she started, "this camp throws a contest at the end of summer called the Horsemanship Olympics. These games are comprised of several events, many of which are common at rodeos. Barrel racing and roping are foremost among them. We will also have a cross-country team race. Some of the counselors wanted to make it a three-legged race but couldn't figure out which legs to tie—the horses, or yours." A lot of the kids laughed at this, including me. Mrs. Karen actually had a pretty good sense of humor.

"The main rule in this race will be riding alongside your partner," she continued. "We'll go into further details later. There will be several other events that we will discuss as well. A few are even individual competitions but can help your team score points. The Horsemanship Olympics will be worth sixty percent of your team's final score. Ten percent will come from your teamwork and behavior throughout the entire summer." She paused after this, waiting for the information to settle in. Like most people, it was easy to do the math in my head and wonder, *what about the other thirty percent?*

"I am telling you all of this now so I can explain what we are about to announce. In the past, we have had the Horsemanship Olympics and overall behavior, and that was where you scored *all* of your points. This year, we have added something new. This event is going to be held two weeks before the Olympics, which means you need to start preparing for it now. This event is called the Trail Trial and will be worth thirty percent of the points."

Whispers broke out across the room. Before the noise could get out of hand, Mrs. Karen spoke again. "This event is called that because it all takes place in the open land of this ranch."

"Yes, your parents knew about this before camp started and signed permission slips," Mrs. Karen said, answering a question from one of the boys up front. "As I was saying, you and your partner will stay out in the open range alone for as long as you can. You are allowed to take supplies you think you will need. Points will be given according to how long you last compared to the rest of the teams. The campers who stay out the longest will not only receive top marks, they will get bonus points to help them get an edge against the other teams in the Olympics.

"That is all I will say on the matter today. Start brainstorming with your partner regarding your plans. The other counselors think you won't last through the weekend. I, on the other hand, disagree. I don't think you'll last twenty-four hours. I would love to be proven wrong. Either way, good luck." With that, she left the pavilion, and the murmur from students turned into a roar.

The campers were buzzing with excitement for the next few days. Most activities carried on the same as usual. We still had the different water sessions every day. We still had the hours we practiced on barrel racing and roping. We even had a few times when counselors took us out into the woods near the barn where the cross-country race would be so we could practice racing with our partner. The ropes course was especially fun because you had to have at least six people per group at a time, which meant Kat and I could hang out and Jackie and Tiffany could hang out. It was a win-win situation.

The remaining days before the competitions passed by quickly, but for once, I wanted them to slow down until I figured out how to survive Jackie. Other than the fact that we had to stay with our partners, and *only* our partners during the Trail Trial, we hadn't heard anything more about the specifics of the challenge. *Come to think of it, no wonder all the partnered groups are two girls or two boys. How did no one see this woody challenge coming?* Many of the campers had asked and pestered the adults at camp, but they had their lips sealed.

The days swept past until the Trail Trial was to begin at two o'clock the next day. A meeting was scheduled for tomorrow at noon to discuss the specifics of the event, and finally, hopefully, we would be getting some answers.

19

Talking Things Out

THAT NIGHT, I took a longer shower than was necessary. After an entire day of dust, heat, and sweat, the cool water and sudsy foam shampoo felt like heaven on my skin. I made myself get out after fifteen minutes. I wasn't going to leave Kat with cold water. She would be sure to return the favor. The towel I brought from home was soft but didn't hold a candle to the soothing water.

After pulling on my pajamas, I wrapped the towel around my hair. I went through the mundane tasks of brushing my teeth, flossing, washing my face, and running a brush through my hair. When I stepped out of the bathroom, Kat was gathering her clothes and going in for her turn.

I remembered the pleasant surprise when I had walked into the cabin for the first time and realized there was a small bathroom in each. They weren't big enough for most cabins to share alone, hence the larger bathroom buildings between the bunk cabins, but they were really nice in the evenings when you didn't want to walk across the camp in your pajamas.

Kat finished quickly and plopped down on my bed where I was reading. I put the fantasy novel down when she asked, "So what's your plan to survive being stuck with Jackie for a weekend or more?"

I fell back onto my bed and spread my arms out by my side. "I have no idea," I groaned. "Sure, I can tolerate an hour or two when we're working, but multiple days on end with only her? I can't imagine keeping myself from killing her," I said, not sure if I was joking or not.

"I'll talk to God about it and ask Him to give you extra patience and good will with her," Kat said solemnly.

"I'll need it," I admitted, staring up at the ceiling. "How about you and Tiffany?" I asked. I needed to change the subject. My bad mood was doing neither of us any good.

"She's actually really good so far. She's soft-spoken and doesn't speak her mind very often. It's a chore to even get her to choose between two things. But she's really smart— like freakishly smart. I think she has a bit of a photographic memory. Tell her something once, or let her read something, and she'll say it all back to you two weeks later."

"Must be handy."

"Too bad she doesn't show it much. You have to be really focused to catch it."

"Hmm."

We stayed up about thirty more minutes, chatting about everything under the stars. We talked about how we thought the trail riding was going to go. We discussed who we thought stood a chance at winning the competition, which team we thought was going to stay out in the wilderness the longest—not counting us of course—and other things.

We would've stayed up all night but both decided we needed all the rest we could get, because the next night we would have no clue where we would be sleeping, if at all. I climbed under the covers as Kat did the same. I called goodnight, said a little prayer, and then closed my eyes. The present world soon faded away and was replaced by a magical world where the limits of reality were no more.

20

Prep Work

TWELVE, WHICH WAS the time the meeting was scheduled to take place, came faster than I wanted it to. Kat and I made sure to get to Big Red well before the crowd began to form. We didn't talk. I figured it was because we were both *way* too nervous. *Is Kat right about Tiffany?* From what I'd seen, Kat and Tiffany were pretty solid in every event. The actual points for each event hadn't been scored yet, but by now, everyone had a feel of who the competition was. If Kat and Tiffany could keep from killing each other this weekend, they would have a pretty good chance at being in the running.

Something squirmed deep in my gut. I didn't mean to be jealous, but I still was. Teaming with Jackie this summer had been an ordeal, to say the least. It seemed we were never meant to get along. I figured I could've tried harder to befriend her, but she certainly didn't make an effort on her end. At 12:15 p.m., everyone finally settled into their seats in the barn. I looked around at many newly familiar faces. There hadn't been many times when we were all in one place at the same time.

As I looked around, I noticed how the number of campers had dwindled. The younger kids had gone home after only two weeks. They weren't old enough for the summer-long schedule. Some of the older kids had only decided to stay for the beginning of summer as well. These had been paired up together so their teams wouldn't affect the scores of those who stayed. The remaining teens were here for the rest of the summer. I counted twenty in all. Ten teams, and I was probably closer to the bottom than the top. *Rats.*

The crowd was tamed when Mr. Wyatt hollered, "Listen up, ya hooligans." A hush fell among the teens almost instantly. Everyone leaned forward as one to catch the slightest sound. "I'm sure you've all heard talk about the Trail Trial we're having, and I'm sure you're anxious to get moving." He paused and surveyed the crowd, as if wondering which kids were going to make it out alive. "There aren't many rules you need to worry about. Each team will be given a cell phone."

A few kids began to murmur. I heard bits and pieces. They didn't know why they had to be given a phone when they already had one. "This phone is programed with several emergency numbers on speed dial as well as the counselors' and the ranch's number." Mr. Wyatt continued like he hadn't heard the kids begin to whisper-shout across the room. "The phone only calls—no texting or Facebook or YouTube. The point of this trial is to test you out on your own. The only other thing the phone has is a tracking device for us to keep tabs on you.

"We will use the phones to call you if we need to check up on you, or you can call us in case of an emergency. If you have a phone or any other electronic device with you, it must be left in your cabin or turned in at the main office where it will be safely stored." The murmurs became an uproar, but only for a moment. When Mr. Wyatt raised his hand for silence, the noise died down considerably.

"The second thing you must know is the boundary line. My property is roughly 700 acres. That is plenty of space for you to roam. You may be anywhere within the fence line. If you go outside, your team will be disqualified." The room had become even more quiet. Everyone stilled, the calm before a major storm. "You must stay with your partner at all times and *only* your partner. No double teaming. And you are allowed to bring anything with you that your horses can carry, except of course, for electronics.

"Important things to remember are food, water, and clothes," he said. "Before you guys leave today, make sure you come up and get one of these." He held up a small device in his hand, like a really short and fat straw. "This is a Sawyer

Mini Water Filter. We have enough for all campers to have their own. Use it. I would rather be overcautious than take a kid to the hospital because they wanted to drink questionable water. This little guy will do most of the hard work for you but do your best to find clear running water or pack some bottled water in your saddlebags."

He looked as if he was about to dismiss us to get ready when he brightened suddenly. "Oh, and I almost forgot." A mischievous smile crossed his lips. "Each team gets a pack horse, or I should probably say, pack pony." As soon as he said this, the barn doors swung open to reveal some of the counselors holding the lead of one or two Shetland ponies. There was one as bright as vanilla ice cream. Another was a pinto, her colors contrasting beautifully on her tiny body. There was a little gelding the color of chocolate. Right next to him was a pitch-black mass of fur and fat.

"Dash," I squealed in realization. I leaped up from my chair and ran across the room at top speed and tackled him in a hug. He nickered in greeting. I could hear quite a few chuckles from several of the kids, but it was muted by the sound of a few other happy campers who were seeing their miniature ponies again.

"As many of you have probably guessed, the ranch didn't own any ponies for the teams," said Mr. Wyatt. "We asked the parents of some of the campers if we could borrow the ponies for a weekend. Some of the ponies were even here at the beginning of the summer for the little kids. We kept those all summer and hid them so y'all wouldn't get suspicious.

"Those of you who own the ponies will have those for the trial. Everyone else can just pick one they like." *So, my parents were in on this and didn't tell me? Oh, they are going to pay for that.* The kids weren't snickering at me anymore. They were swiftly walking to the other ponies to try and find the best ones before they were taken. I buried my face in Dash's neck. He smelled of sweet grass. I smiled into him. Maybe we stood a chance at winning, after all.

"You don't expect us to take *that* thing with us, do you?" It took me almost no time to place the voice with the name. I turned to look up into the scowling face of Jackie.

"What's wrong with Dash?" I asked, incredulous.

"He's *way* fat, he looks like a dog, and there is no way we can do anything around all that hair," she complained.

"I've never had trouble with his hair before," I countered. "And he's not too fat, he's a *Shetland.* Also, why do you think he looks even remotely like a dog?" She rolled her eyes at me, a look that I had learned to interpret as "my time would be wasted trying to explain it to you." She stalked off to her cabin with only the instruction to meet her at the main corral by two over her shoulder. "It's okay, boy. She'll warm up to you," I crooned.

Dash nickered his agreement. "Who could resist a cute little guy like me?"

The next hour and a half were stressful to say the least. I grabbed the water filters and phone for our group. Then I packed most of what I thought I would need, but I kept thinking of something else I needed and had to take out stuff to fit it. The hardest part was situating everything into a space that was as small as possible. I only needed to make Chance carry what would fit in my saddle bags, a small tent and sleeping bag strapped on top of the saddle bags, and two canteens of water which hung from the saddle horn.

Any more than that would tire him out way too quickly and slow Jackie and me down. I decided Dash would carry the food and water filters Jackie and I would share in an extra set of saddle bags I had borrowed from the tack room. It took me three loads to get everything to the barn where the horses were tied. The counselors were able to help get our horses caught and tied up as well as give a little bit of advice, but other than that they had been instructed to leave us to our own devices. They were only to supervise. This was either going to be really fun or extremely dangerous. My guess was that it would end up being hilarious to some extent or another.

I plopped the last bag down beside Chance and retrieved a spare brush from the tack room. On my way back, I looked around to see if Jackie was here yet. I couldn't see her, but only about half the campers were here so far so I wasn't worried. I brushed Chance swiftly and efficiently and then went to work on Dash. He took a little longer than Chance. Chance may have been bigger, but Dash had him beat in sheer amount of hair. I finished up with both my boys in another five minutes.

I grabbed the saddle pad for Chance and slapped it against my right leg a few times. Stray dust billowed into the air and left the saddle pad much cleaner than before. Then I aligned the saddle pad onto Chance's back and made sure it was straight. I picked up the saddle next and heaved it up and onto Chance's back, setting it down gently. While I was securing the girth underneath Chance, a set of boots came into view. Old and worn-out with scuff marks, the boots were well used, and I would recognize them anywhere.

"Nervous much?" a male voice asked. I finished with the girth before looking up. Blue eyes showed curiosity and authentic concern, but the half smile on his lips was nothing but mischievous.

"Not too bad," I answered. "But I would feel a lot better if I got to trade partners. What do ya say, bud?"

Austin's laugh was sharp and loud. "Not in a million years, Hope. I've got a good partner, and I don't care if Jackie has decent horsemanship skills, I wouldn't team with her if I was paid. Not with her attitude."

"She'd probably do anything for you, the attractive cowboy who doesn't talk to her much." I batted my eyelashes flirtatiously and put my hands together in a pleading way. I was doing my best Jackie imitation, and from the looks of Austin, I was spot on. He shuffled his feet and rubbed the back of his neck. He was as nervous as I'd ever seen him. But anyone in their right mind who caught the attention of a girl like Jackie would be. It only took a minute for his regular smile and easygoing stance to reappear.

"You think I'm attractive?" he asked, grinning cheekily. It was my turn to be uncomfortable. I could feel the blush creeping up the sides of my face, and I prayed Austin didn't notice.

"I'm just quoting the certifiably insane," I shot back. He answered by taking his hat off and whacking me atop the head with it. Which reminded me, I needed to get my hat before we left. I didn't always wear it because it had a tendency of falling off my head, but we were going to be out in the weather nonstop for the next couple of days, so my hat was essential. Austin smiled at me once more before turning to focus his attention on Blitz, who was only two horses away from Chance.

I worked quickly to get Dash and Chance completely situated. After I finished, I checked around to see if Jackie had finally graced me with her presence. My gaze didn't spot her this time either, though I noticed almost everyone else was here working on getting ready. At this rate, we were going to get out on the trail last, and all the best spots for camping would be taken. Technically, the beginning of the Trail Trial started at two, but if we left early, it was fair game. We just had to leave close to two o'clock or get deducted points for being late. Still, there wasn't much I could do until she showed up. I dashed quickly toward my cabin to grab my hat. If Jackie didn't show herself by the time I got back, I would start saddling her horse up myself. I knew what her tack looked like anyway: shiny, clean and bedazzled.

I was out of breath when I got back. Jackie was standing beside her horse, swinging a canteen in her hand while a boy with dark eyes and shaggy hair set her bags down in front of her. He looked older, maybe seventeen, and probably thought Jackie was his age with how much makeup she was wearing. Jackie said something to him I didn't hear, and he left to go work on his own horse. As I reached her and looked at her pile of bags, my eyebrows quirked up.

"Is that all your stuff?" I asked.

"Yes," she huffed, offended. "Did you think I was going to be one of those girls who had twenty bags wherever I go?"

I didn't want her to be right, but that was exactly what I thought was going to happen. The nightmare of a pile of bags burying Dash alive kept me up much of the night. But the pile in front of me was pretty small. I didn't want to admit I was impressed.

My look must've given me away because Jackie continued. "Well, obviously, the situation is less than desirable, seeing as I had to leave my blow-dryer and curling iron behind. But this is a competition of horsemanship and professionalism. I'm sure even you understand that. Anyway, I will be roughing it long enough to win, and then it will be right back to how it should be, where I smell like vanilla and coffee beans instead of grass and dirt."

"Okay," I said. The word came out short and stiff. I had not been ready for this side of Jackie. Maybe this wasn't going to be as bad as I thought.

21

Truce

BY THE TIME Jackie and I were ready, six teams had already left. We wouldn't be last, but I'd hoped that the delay was because the other teams got anxious to leave and forgot something. Supplies were an important part of the first leg of the Trail Trial. The other part was teamwork with your partner, the horses, and the outdoors. That was why, when we got into the massive acreage that would be the boundaries, I didn't object when Jackie took the lead and headed north toward a place I believed to have a stream and lots of trees and brush. I didn't have any better ideas of where to head, and the idea of arguing with Jackie this early in the trial didn't seem wise. I just hoped she knew where she was going.

After a short while of awkward silence, I was fed up with it. The quiet was unnerving. "So, what's the plan?" I started. "Food and water are important. And it needs to be *running* water. I'm not really in a pond-water drinking mood. We also need to find shelter. Of course, we have our tents, but I would feel better if we found a cave or an outcropping of rocks to provide us with most of the protection if the weather decides to be cruel to us. What do you think about—"

"Are you going to be yammering like this the entire time? I'm warning you, I brought Duct Tape in case of an emergency." She had a smile on her face, but the look of disdain in her green eyes muffled it. She turned quickly back to focus on the horizon. So fast actually, that her ponytail of blonde and pink hair swung behind her like a whip. I clucked to Chance to get him at a trot until I came up beside Jackie and her palomino. Dash had to lope to catch up.

"Look, I know you didn't want me as a partner this summer. Believe me, the feeling is mutual." She opened her mouth but didn't comment. "But we can both agree on the matter that we hate losing, and definitely don't want to come in dead last. So, maybe, we need to find a way to tolerate each other for the next couple of days."

"Truce then, I guess." She looked at me when she said it. And this time, there was nothing that showed malice in her face or posture. There was nothing showing she liked me either, but it was a lot better than it had been.

"Truce," I agreed. "Hey, can we slow down a little? Poor Dash is going to be tired out in the first fifteen minutes if we keep him at this pace." Jackie looked back at Dash who was loping valiantly behind the bigger horses. He puffed out a grunt and stretched his tiny legs as far as they would reach.

"I guess we should slow our pace a little," she relented. "It's not like he can do much about his stubby legs."

As we continued to ride farther into the open lands of the ranch, we passed several teams. Most of them I recognized but didn't know the names of. I caught a glimpse of Austin and Zeke headed off to the right of us. From what I could tell, they were headed toward the mountain range, higher ground than us. I kept my eyes out for Kat but didn't see her. The flatter ground we were riding on had started to slant down, and trees closed in on us.

As Jackie led the way, I noticed how calm she was. She seemed to be perfectly content out here in the middle of nowhere. Her shoulders were more relaxed, and it was quiet enough to hear her breathing, deep and slow. "Do you go riding out in the woods often?" She seemed startled by my sudden question but didn't snap at me.

"The woods have a funny way of calming people, no matter who they are," she said. She didn't elaborate, and I didn't push the subject. Whatever she was feeling, I didn't want to rile her up again. This peaceful Jackie was a much better person to be around than the Jackie I had seen this summer.

Mom always said the bad people were that way because they were shaped by the people around them; they were scuffed up and broken from being tossed around too much, and eventually, they quit trying to be good. I wondered if Jackie had anything happen in her life that made her calloused and stuck-up. I didn't think it was okay to act like a pig when you'd been hurt, but it definitely gave a reason of why.

I looked at my watch when I realized I'd lost track of time. I had no idea how long it would be until it was dark and we could no longer see. The green numbers glowed steadily: 6:38. It would be dark in another hour or so.

"I think it's time we probably set up camp and get some food." As soon as I said it, my stomach growled in agreement. I had been so lost in thought I had forgotten about it. I looked out to my left, where Jackie rode about thirty feet from me. She looked up from something she was staring at in front of her and directed her attention to me.

"Anywhere around here look promising for a campsite?" It took me a minute to realize she had asked my opinion for the first time since we started this trial four or five hours ago.

"Um." I thought about it. "A couple minutes back, I saw a huge pile of boulders with some overhangings. There were also several bigger trees with branches covering the area. We could use them as a shield from the rain, and the river was only a couple hundred yards away from that so we would have fresh water."

"I suppose it is the best option to turn up thus far," she begrudgingly admitted. She pulled her horse around, and I did the same with Chance and Dash. It didn't take us long to reach the spot I'd described.

I slipped off Chance in what I hoped was a swift and graceful move, but what was probably a wobbly mess. That was what riding for over four hours straight did to me. I tied Chance to a nearby tree that stood a hundred yards or so from the future campsite. I left Dash tied to Chance's saddle horn. He was tuckered out and stood obediently quiet. I grabbed the sleeping bag first and then got the tent on the second load.

Setting up was pretty easy. The small size of the tent left little room for error. The spot I chose for my tent had a bigger, mostly flat rock hanging over it. I had climbed up on top of the rock before setting up the tent and jumped up and down on it to ensure its stability. After finishing with the tent, I stuffed the sleeping bag inside, and went back to my boys to grab my saddle bags next. They were filled with clothes, a bar of soap, a roll of toilet paper, and a few other odds and ends. I stowed them, still packed, into my tent. Jackie was doing much the same thing a few feet from me.

"I'm going to go water Chance and Dash," I said, trying to start a conversation. I mean, I didn't want to argue with her all day, but a few words here and there would not be unwelcome.

"Take Sugarfoot with you," she said when I had almost reached the horses. I looked back at her, and she must have known by my look that ordering me around wasn't a good way to keep the truce we'd made. "She won't drink well by herself in a new environment," she continued, partially mending her previous statement. I turned back toward the horses. I'd let it slide. She must have been trying just as hard, or maybe harder, than me. *Dear God, help me to show her kindness and patience. I know I can only do it with your help, because I am seriously lacking in the patience department.*

I reached out, untied Dash, and looped his lead around Chance's neck and tied it loosely. I then untied Chance. I took a few steps toward Sugarfoot. She looked at me skeptically for a moment like she was thinking, *this scrawny little creature is going to lead me?* But then she resigned herself to me leading her with Chance and Dash toward the river.

"Would you mind getting some firewood while I get the horses watered?" I asked, in what I hoped was a kind but don't-mess-with-me voice.

"Sure," came the reply. I heard the crunch of leaves, signaling that she was keeping her word in finding kindling.

The river was almost too small to have that name, but it was frolicking in happy chorus. The rocks in the bed were smooth and clean, washed by the constant flow of the water. When we reached the edge, Chance and Sugarfoot dropped their heads to drink contentedly from the water. Dash didn't even hesitate an instant. He jumped right into the stream.

The water came up almost to his belly. He drank and then splashed around, enjoying the cold, refreshing water. I was glad I had already taken his pack off. Otherwise, all of our food would have been soggy.

I dropped Chance and Sugarfoot's leads on the ground, knowing they weren't going anywhere. I left Dash tied to Chance though. He seemed a little too hyper right now to be unsupervised. I turned to my right and petted Chance on his broad shoulder. The skin quivered beneath my touch. It felt weird. A talent I'd always wanted to be able to do was move my skin like the horses could. They used it to keep off the flies, but I thought it added character to them, another little way they communicated with each other.

Snap.

I swung my head around, toward the other side of the river, to get a look at what made the sound. I saw nothing, well, nothing that could've caused the noise I heard. A few birds chirped in a tree, and a squirrel ran up a different tree, but other than that, the woods were still. I turned my attention back to Chance. I ran my hands down to the girth wrapped around his belly. I unhooked the strap from the latch and loosened it up a couple of notches. Chance pulled in a deep breath and sighed in absolute, calm joy. I moved around to Sugarfoot and proceeded to give her the same treatment. She pushed against my hand, eager to be more comfortable too.

As the horses finished filling themselves, I grabbed the canteens that were still strapped to the saddle horns and topped them off. I made a mental note to remind Jackie that we would have to start drinking through the filter straws now that our canteens weren't just tap water.

After the horses had all they wanted, we meandered back to the campsite. In our absence, Jackie had made a reasonable pile of kindling with a few big sticks of wood stacked beside it. She had also found several smaller rocks to use as a circle barrier for the fire. The girl kept surprising me. The next thing I knew, she'd be sitting across from me by the fire telling me all about her days in the Girl Scouts. I smiled at the thought. Maybe there was more to this Jackie King than met the eye.

Dinner was a small affair. Neither of us were very hungry, so we munched on some beef jerky and granola bars. The fire was warm and relaxing after being in the saddle all afternoon. It had a way of making someone feel like curling up for a nice long sleep.

As the sun set and the shadows appeared around us, I got a strange sense of déjà vu. Things hadn't gone well the last time I had been out in the woods at night by myself. *This isn't last summer though. You have a partner. You are allowed to be here. The camp can watch out for you with the tracker.* I shook the thoughts away. There was no need to worry. Nothing bad was going to happen.

After dinner, we unsaddled the horses and took the tack into our tents for protection in the event of rain. We gave all three of the horses a good scratching after a long afternoon of riding which they thoroughly enjoyed.

Lastly, we hooked the horses up to their stakes to keep them from going on any adventures while we were sleeping. They didn't seem to mind their fifteen-foot radius much, since they all immediately went down on their backs and rolled around. I thought I heard Jackie laughing at the horses' antics, but when I turned to look at her, she avoided me by going to her tent and saying she was tired.

So, maybe we weren't going to get along, but perhaps this truce thing was going to work out in the end. That was what life was all about, right? Putting up with people you didn't like. I thought Jackie and I were going to make this work out just fine. It was, after all, already the end of the first day of the Trail Trial. I made sure the fire was safely put out and headed to my tent.

As I was climbing into it, I heard a familiar sound—a sing-song call on the winds. It was a horse. *Not Sugarfoot, Dash, or Chance, it's too far away for that. But maybe Calypso or Blitz? Were they close enough for me to hear? Not likely.* My mind was probably just playing tricks on me. I needed some sleep, that was all. I crawled the rest of the way into the tent, zipped it up, and tried to shut out the sounds of my mind playing the call again and again in my head—the sound of a horse that shouldn't be here.

22

Routine

I WOKE UP the next morning feeling stiff from sleeping on the hard ground but was also refreshed by the scent of the forest. I had never come across anything that smelled quite as good as early morning in a forest when the dew from the leaves the night before hadn't dried up yet. I breathed in deeply, my lungs filling with fresh air that woke me up better than coffee or sugary cereal. I crawled out of my tent and stood upright. Raising my hands above my head and twisting to either side, I stretched the soreness out of my limbs. I let my arms fall to my sides and rolled my shoulders and then my neck, relishing in the feeling of the popping. When I had rolled my neck to both sides and it stopped cracking, I felt like I could actually stand straight again. I popped some of my knuckles for good measure.

Feeling more awake, I slipped on my boots, grabbed all the canteens and headed toward the stream. Jackie was still in her tent asleep, but if she woke up and needed me, I'd be close enough to hear her yell. The woods were a little louder this morning. The birds were chirping in the trees, and small woodland creatures were going about their business of the day. They must have thought I was a funny creature, what with my messy bedhead and my pajama pants and old T-shirt. *Pajamas and boots. Yup, that just about summed me up.*

When I made it to the stream, I filled the canteens up with the clear water and then pulled my filter straw from my pocket. It only took a few sips to quench my overnight thirst. I splashed a little on my face. The water was cold and refreshing on my skin. I was fully awake now. The first thing I noticed were several fat fish swimming lazily in the stream. They looked about how I felt this morning: sleepy. The second thing I noticed was that my stomach had awakened from its slumber and reminded me I was hungry. *It must be breakfast time.* I headed back to the campsite.

Jackie was crawling out of her tent when I got back. She was dressed much the same as me, in pajama shorts and a comfy T-Shirt. She pulled a hoodie on when she got out of her tent. The only difference between my attire and hers was that her hair was elegantly braided up in a rose shape on the side of her head. She had braided her hair in such a way that it looked like it wouldn't fall out for a few days, and the pink streaks in her hair made the flower look real, just pinned in her hair. I had to admit that it looked really good. It almost made me wish I could braid cool things into my hair, almost.

"I got the canteens refilled," I told her, which I guess seemed obvious because I was carrying the canteens and had just come back from the direction of the stream. I just wanted to start a conversation that didn't involve us arguing. Water seemed like a safe topic. She nodded at the firepit.

"What are we having for breakfast?" she asked. The tone in her voice seemed genuinely curious, not like she expected me to get breakfast ready on my own.

"I packed granola bars and some fruit," I offered. Again, she nodded. She turned and shuffled around in her tent for a few moments and produced a box of honey cheerios. She held it out in front of her like an offering.

"I couldn't bring any milk, so we'll have to eat it dry. But the box is almost full, so we won't run out for a few days."

"That'll work great," I assured her. I walked over to my tent to retrieve my contribution to the breakfast meal. We ate in silence.

"I'm going to take a walk in the woods for a little bit," Jackie said after finishing her breakfast.

"Okay," I replied.

"Not going to stop me? Protest a little?"

"I don't see why. All we have to do is stay away from civilization longer than the other teams. No one said what we have to do while we're out here except not die." It looked like she was about to speak. But then she must have thought *why bother?* "Just make sure you don't wander off too far," I called after her. "We still have to use the buddy system." She turned around in time to see my air quotes when I mentioned not separating from each other. She probably knew I was as serious as I was joking.

For the next hour, I massaged Dash, Chance, and Sugarfoot, who were having a swell time just eating and dozing. I also sat down and read for a while. Actually, it might have been longer than an hour. I tended to lose track of time when I was reading. But a while later, Jackie came back into the clearing.

"Have a nice walk?" I asked her pleasantly. Reading tended to put me in a good mood. Unless it was a sad book, then it was better not to interact with me.

"Pretty good," she said simply.

"What were you doing?"

"Just thinking."

It was silent for a few moments. Neither of us knew what to say now. This truce thing may have been working out, but it sure was a lot less interesting. I didn't know if that was a good or a bad thing.

"So, what are we going to do about lunch?" Jackie asked. This time, she was the one to find common ground: food.

"I packed several bags of chips and snacks. I also made about five peanut butter and jelly sandwiches. They won't go bad very fast in Ziplocs." I answered.

"I brought basically the same thing," she said. "We need to last longer than a few days to win this thing, but we don't have enough food for that." She hummed and tapped her foot, thinking hard. "We need to find a way to eat only one sandwich apiece a day and breakfast foods should be rationed too."

"But we can't very well starve ourselves," I pointed out.

"There has to be a way," Jackie insisted, frowning slightly.

"Call me crazy," I said, grinning, "but I think I have an idea." I jumped up and started looking around for the best spot to start searching. I made it all the way around the campsite when I saw a potential spot. Behind the mounds of rocks we had been sleeping beside, was an area that didn't get a lot of sunlight and had lots of leaves from years of the tree residing above it.

I fell to my knees and dug in the soft dirt and leaves. My fingers sunk into the mulch and raked it away. My eyes did not spot them instantly, but when I sifted the dirt again, I found several. I picked one of the creatures up between my thumb and pointer finger.

"Earthworms," Jackie shrieked. She was bent over closer to me than I had realized, and when she screamed, she nearly busted my left eardrum. "There is no way you are getting me to eat earthworms. I would do a lot of things to win, but you have crossed the line."

"Calm down, Jackie," I said. "The worms are just the bait."

"Bait?" she asked. "Are you going to try to fish? From where?"

"I saw some fish in the stream today. They were a good size for a meal or two. When we can't catch any more, we'll move on to another part of the ranch where there will be more fish."

"And how do you expect to catch the fish?" she asked skeptically. I noticed she didn't say *we* this time. I think I might have been pushing my luck a bit.

"I'm working on it," I tell her.

Fifteen minutes later, I was ready to test my theory. I didn't have anything to improvise a fishing pole, but I saw something else on TV once that I was going to try out. I had taken my knife and tied it tightly and carefully to the end of a five-foot-long stick. I gathered up a pile of worms and placed them on a big rock so they would not wiggle away too quickly. *Yup, I was going to skewer us some fish.* Why did I carry a knife, some people might wonder? *Well, I needed to be protected and armed, didn't I?* My dad had gotten it for me two years ago on my twelfth birthday.

The knife was seven inches long from sharp tip to smooth wooden handle. My name was carved in beautiful cursive on one side. My dad had also given me a soft leather sleeve with a clip on the end of it. I carried it clipped on the inside of my right boot, and no one was the wiser.

"I'll get the fish caught if you can get a fire going," I said to Jackie, who had just been watching me in horror and disgust. She seemed a little better when I gave her an out from catching fish. "When I get back, we're going to have a fish fry." I grabbed my weapon and positioned it in the crook of my arm for easy carrying. I scooped up the worms and went out to put my plan into action.

When I got close to the stream, I slowed my brisk walk into a cautious creeping motion. I didn't want to scare off my dinner. This was going to be hard enough without adding senseless noise to the mix. I crouched down low beside the lazily flowing river. The worms were set carefully in a pile on a rock beside me. I set my spear down and took off my shoes and socks. I set them far enough away where the water couldn't get to them and then rolled up my pants to my knees. Speaking of my pants, *why was I still in pajamas?* I thought. *Why not?* My brain replied. *It's not like they're super skimpy or embarrassing.* "Good point," I muttered to myself.

I finished with my pants and quickly dipped my toes in. The water was warmer than this morning because the sun had been shining through the treetops for a couple hours, but it was still cold. I bit my lip to keep from jerking away. No doubt, the sudden movement would scare away the fish I'd spotted several feet away.

The rocks were smooth from the caress of the river, and they were clear of slime and moss. I stood up slowly to get my balance before moving. The cold water came up to my knees. The rocks I was standing on had been constantly smoothed over by the water, which meant they were super easy to slip on, and I couldn't afford to make a mistake like falling today. I carefully leaned over and grabbed my spear and got a good grip on it in my right hand. With my left hand, I grabbed a handful of the worms.

Moving slowly, I slid my feet in the direction of the fish. I did not pick my feet up but an inch. The rest of my body was stiff and unmoving. I got to where I was three feet from the nearest fish and stopped. The fish showed no signs of seeing me. Three of them swam in slow circles from one side of the stream to another. They were upstream from me, so the current naturally pulled them in my direction. I stared at them intently and gripped my spear harder. With my left hand, I reached out and slowly dropped four or five worms close to the fish. One of them darted closer to see what new food had come their way. Soon, the other two joined the first.

I counted to three in my head and then, with a swift movement, stabbed the biggest fish in the head, pinning it to the rocky streambed. The other two fish darted off faster than my eyes could follow, but I focused on the fish I had stabbed. I bent down and grabbed its tail firmly before taking the spear out of its eye. I grinned in triumph. *My plan actually worked.* But it needed to work one more time. One fish, even if it was a foot long like the one I just killed, was not big enough for two girls surviving on granola bars.

I was about to climb out of this part of the river and go look for another spot where the fish weren't expecting me when I noticed a lone fish swimming my way, fifteen feet upstream. I crept as fast as I could to the rock where a few worms still lay. I set the dead fish down on the rock and grabbed the remaining worms. With my ammunition restocked, I got back into my original position and waited for the fish to get closer. This one was a little shorter, but thicker and fatter. Its scales gleamed in the sun and darkened when it swam somewhere with more shadow.

It was seven feet away now. Six feet. Five feet. I contemplated tossing the bait in the water like I did last time, but this fish looked more skittish and swift. With a jerk of its tail, it shot forward a bit. It was right beside me now. I was counting to myself in my mind when it shot forward at a rapid pace. Before it could escape, I stabbed at it. I pinned its tail haphazardly. Before it could wiggle away, I dropped the worms and lunged at it.

Cold water splashed in my face, and the water soaked the front of my shirt and most of my pants. I grabbed the fish and firmly pinned it to the bottom of the riverbed. With one hand, I held it tight and with the other I jabbed it quickly in the head to kill it. Blood billowed in the water for a moment but then was washed away. I grabbed the now dead fish by its mouth and carried it over to the other one. I set the fish by the other and worked for a minute or two to try and squeeze the water out of my pants and part of my shirt. When I'd accomplished all I could, I grabbed the spear and the two fish and headed back to the campsite with fish sticks on my mind.

Jackie must have had some faith in me, or was just really hungry, because she not only had a nice-sized fire going but had the tin skillet we had brought out and ready. The horses had been moved a little farther off to give them fresh grass to munch on, so they were taken care of as well. Jackie had a genuine smile on her face when she saw me.

"You sure got down and dirty," she commented, "or rather, down and wet." She grabbed the skillet and placed it on a rock that stood in the center of the firepit. Jackie had built the fireplace in such a way that the fire heated the rock without getting smoke and bark on it.

"The skillet should be heated up pretty quick," Jackie said. "How long will it take you to skin those fish?"

"Not long," I answered and set to work to do just that. I took the fish and laid them on a boulder near the fire. The rock was set up to be my chair, but I'd have to sit on the ground today. I took my spear and untied my knife from it. Placing the knife beside the fish, I strode over to my tent to find the rest of the supplies I would need.

I retrieved a bar of soap from my saddle bags and grabbed my canteen too. While I was at my tent, I quickly changed out of my damp pajamas. On my way back out of the tent, I hung my wet clothes on a tree limb to let them dry. Back at the temporary fish fileting table, I used the water and soap to clean and disinfect a section of the rock. I cleaned my knife as well. Now came the easy part. I had been fishing many times throughout my lifetime. When I was twelve, it was my turn to clean my own fish for our supper. Dad always watched of course, but it was my job to clean the fish I caught, and he would clean his.

I worked carefully to save as much of the meat as I could. When I was done with the first fish, I called Jackie over with the skillet and gave her the meat. She worked on cooking the first fish while I went to work skinning the second one. It took us about thirty minutes to get the meal ready, and by then, it was almost 2:30 in the afternoon. The fish tasted really good. I didn't know if I was just really hungry or if I was proud that we had made it all ourselves or what, but it was *good*. We cleaned the skillet and the two plates we had used and laid down in the sun for a nap. *Who knew planning an entire meal, finding it, catching it, and then cooking it could be so tiring?*

That evening, we talked about what our plan would be for the next day.

"I don't like sitting around in the same spot for very long," Jackie said. "How about we move campsites? Find something besides fish to eat?"

"You don't like the fish I caught us?" I cried dramatically, trying to sound offended.

"They were fine. I just don't like the idea of having them for multiple days in a row."

"Good point. But do you have a better idea?"

"Maybe somewhere with berries we could eat. I heard talk around the ranch about wild blueberries."

"I don't like the idea of eating berries," I said quickly, shutting her down. "What if we eat something poisonous? I'm not good at spotting different plants. With my luck, we're bound to run into something that'll kill me."

"That's why I like the idea of looking for berries," Jackie commented in a bitter tone.

I threw a jibe back at her. "If I die, you'll be disqualified for not having a partner, and you'll have to live with the fact that you killed your only chance of winning the Horsemanship Olympics."

Her face was quite priceless. "Touché," she muttered.

Before a civil war could break out between us, I said, "We can move the campsite though. A change of scenery will keep us busy and not worried about how long we've been out here."

Jackie's face calmed a bit.

"And if we find berries, and we know they are absolutely not poisonous, I guess it would be nice to have some fresh fruit," I added. I wanted to keep this truce thing going, and that meant compromising.

"What time do you want to head out?" Jackie asked me.

"I don't think we should go tonight. It'll be dark shortly after we get packed up and on our way. I don't want to have to find a campsite in the dark. How about first thing in the morning?" I suggested. I was waiting for her to argue, but she didn't. She just nodded in agreement. She only added that she didn't want to wake up early, just whatever time she happened to get up. I agreed with her.

That evening, we walked our horses around for a little while to stretch their legs. I told Chance the plans for tomorrow, and he listened intently, even though he probably couldn't understand a word I was saying. I caught Jackie doing the same to Sugarfoot, leading me to believe we had more in common than I gave us credit for. Dash plodded along behind us, paying more attention to flowers we passed than us.

We tied the horses in their final spot for the night, and they went to munching on the grass contentedly. Jackie and I had peanut butter and jelly sandwiches and then went to bed early. I snuggled in my sleeping bag, about to fall asleep. *How many teams were still out there? Would we see any of them tomorrow? What had happened to the mare I hadn't seen all summer? Where is she? Is she doing okay? Is she fully recovered?* I wanted to see her again. *But how can I find her?* I would try and look first thing when I got home. My eyes were getting heavier by the minute, and as I laid there, sleep reached out for me. The four horses nickered goodnight to each other.

"I miss you so much, Raindancer," I murmured as I drifted off to sleep.

23

Trekking Through Trees

THAT NIGHT, I woke up several times from weird noises. First, a hoot like an owl. The second time was some bushes crunching and rustling. The third time, it was something rubbing up against the tent. I opened my tent door-flap, but nothing out of the ordinary was around, even when I shone a flashlight. Something moved away and off into the distance. *Where is it coming from?*

After a while, the sound quieted down. *I guess it's gone. I can finally get some sleep.* I stayed awake another hour. *What was outside my tent?* It probably wasn't dangerous. If it was, the horses would've woken us up when they tried to run and remembered they were tied to stakes. But I was still really curious about what it could've been.

When morning came, I woke up to a cloudy day. The sun was blocked by the cumulonimbus and stratus clouds, and there wasn't a foot of ground that wasn't covered in shade. The good news was that the clouds didn't look dark. I didn't think we'd see more than a light misting today. Jackie and I got up and out of our tents dressed and ready about the same time.

We talked a little about where we wanted to ride today and settled on getting out of the woods. We were going to try and find an open spot where we could sleep under the stars, but that was also at the edge of a forest so there would be more protection if necessary. We needed to have a source of water close by as well. Even if we didn't fish again, we'd need more water for the horses and ourselves.

We ate a hurried breakfast of dry cereal and granola bars and got everything packed up. Before saddling the horses, we took them to the stream so they could get hydrated. We filled up all our canteens while we were at it.

Back at camp it only took a few short minutes to strap all the tack back on the horses and we were ready to go. I swung up on Chance and grabbed Dash's rope. He was the only one of our horses who seemed bummed about leaving. But then again, he never really wanted to exercise. His legs were way too short for it. We headed north, not back the way we came, but away from the stream and the direction we had been traveling two days ago. *Two days ago? Had it really been that long? We've been doing pretty well so far.* But we also had no way of knowing how well everyone else was doing either.

We left the campsite at 9:15 a.m. and it had been almost three hours now. We had trekked through more trees than I could count, crossed several valleys and climbed up a few steep hills. I was getting hungry, and Dash was likely getting tired. He kept making these grunting and squealing noises, protesting the work he was having to partake in.

"Maybe we should take a break for an hour and get lunch? It would give the horses time to catch their breath," I suggested.

"I think Fuzzy would like that," Jackie replied.

"That's not his name."

"But he is fuzzy. Call it a nickname."

"Fine. At least you didn't pick something offensive. Dash loves his long hair." Dash nickered in agreement. His fuzziness made him a hit with all the six to eight-year-old girls. They gave him sugar, so he was loyal to them.

We parked ourselves under a lone oak tree in the middle of a wide stretch of beautiful yellowing grass. The first thing I did after I swung off Chance was unbuckle his girth and loosen it a few notches. He blew a big breath out of his nose and shook all over, like he greatly appreciated a little relaxation. Jackie did the same to Sugarfoot. I heard her nicker contentedly.

We hadn't been riding for a really long time, but with their full equipment, supplies, a rider, and the heat of summer, they got tired more quickly than usual. I took Dash's whole pack off for the break. As soon as it was off, he got down on his knees and rolled over on his back. Then he rolled onto his side and spread his legs out to their full extent—which wasn't really that long—and I swear he smiled. *What a ham.*

Since we needed to make this a relatively quick break, we ate sandwiches for lunch and decided to find camp early in the afternoon so we could scrounge up something for dinner. When we set off again, I looked up at the cloudy sky and was grateful for the overcast. It may have been hot now, but it would've been a whole lot worse if the sun was out and shining.

We trekked for another two hours until Jackie pointed out a spot that looked promising. It was a patch of flat ground with short green grass. Part of the trees from the forest close by pulled out into a semicircle around the area. From the sound my ears were feeding me, there must have been running water close by somewhere as well. The only problem? Two riders were trotting off in the distance, a miniature pony following behind. Another team was headed in the same direction as us. *Great.* After two days of peace and tranquility, we were probably going to get in a fight for the softest ground to sleep on or something. And by we, I meant Jackie. She was super possessive of her soft ground.

It took a few minutes for me to distinguish who the other riders were. To my complete horror, it was Harley, Jackie's *best friend.* Forget possibly losing our new campsite. I was about to lose nice Jackie.

Jackie was thrilled to see Harley. When she recognized her, she urged Sugarfoot into a canter to reach her faster. Harley did the same. They started chatting and squealing, telling each other all about what had been happening to them recently. I took this time to look at Harley's partner. She was still a little ways off, but I could see her clearly enough to know that I hadn't seen her much at Cowboy Camp, though I recognized her. She had chin-length chocolate-colored hair and tan skin, proof of her many hours outside. As we pulled up to each other, she extended her hand and said, "My name's Kinzie."

"Hope," I said, shaking her hand. About that time, I got the news I had been dreading.

"Great news, Hope. Harley and Kinzie are going to stay with us tonight." Kinzie quirked an eyebrow when she heard that. She was probably thinking the exact thing I was.

"Jackie, isn't that against the rules?" I pointed out. "We aren't supposed to pair up with other groups. That kind of defeats the purpose of arranged partners." I didn't want to get on her bad side by suggesting her idea was stupid, but I'd been raised to follow the rules. Not that it happened all the time, but I tried my best.

"Oh, stop worrying. They'll never know." She laughed.

"Trackers in the phones sounds like they're smart enough to know that two groups staying close to each other overnight are teaming up," I shot back at her, meaner than intended.

"We'll just tie the phone in a bag and put it up in a tree. We'll pick a spot a couple minutes ride from there and then go pick it up later," Harley argued. *Really? I knew this kid was a punk. It must've come from her dark spiky hair, her superior attitude, and her total disregard for authority.* I needed to get Jackie away from Harley before it was too late. *But how am I supposed to do that? Kinzie doesn't seem to care either way, which means I'm the "stick in the mud" for this posse.*

What should I do? On one hand, if I let Jackie get her way, we'd be breaking the rules. On the other, I would have to deal with evil Jackie for the rest of the summer if I got my way.

"How about we hang out for a few hours and then split up? That way we're not really breaking the rules by teaming up, because the teams would only be passing by, but you two have time to catch up," I offered. Man, I had been in the same vicinity as another team for five minutes and already felt like I had hives up and down my arms.

"Fine," Jackie relented.

Turns out, by "split up" Jackie heard fifty yards. That was the farthest I could get our campsites. Kenzie erected one campsite, and I took care of the other. Jackie and Harley were gossiping it up, completely oblivious to the work they were missing out on. Neither of them even noticed when

Kenzie and I took all the supplies off the horses they were *still on*. When I was done setting up camp an hour later, I was getting hungry, and all I could think about were berries. I walked over to the other campsite where Kinzie was.

"You didn't happen to see a patch or two of wild blueberries while you were with Harley, did you?" I asked Kinzie.

"Sure, we did," she replied. "There's a whole lot of them in a valley not far from here. It'd take about seven minutes to ride to, but there are a lot of ripe berries that I saw."

"Great. Can you tell me where they are?" I asked her.

"Nah, I'm not good at directions. You'd get lost. But Harley would know the way," she replied. "Hey, Harley," Kinzie called, directing her voice toward the two girls on horseback. "Hope's thinking about blueberries for dinner. Reckon you can remember how to get there?" She had to yell to get herself heard over Jackie's yammering.

"Sure. Jackie and I can go get some," she hollered back.

"I'll go too," I said, a little too quickly. I knew that if Jackie and Harley went, they'd take forever to get enough berries for all of us to eat. I also didn't like the idea of leaving my teammate, no matter how chill everyone else was with it. "How about you come too, Kinzie? We'll get all the berries we need faster that way, and we won't be out after dark."

"Nope. You guys can go looking for berries. I don't care for getting pricked by a thousand needle-sharp thorns for a handful of fruit. I'll just chill here and eat something I brought. I have one of the phones too, I'll be fine."

I didn't like it. But the way Kinzie said it gave me no choice in the matter. She was patronizing me, but I wasn't going to let it get to me.

"We'll be back in an hour," I promised. It seemed that I now had to keep three girls alive. *Joy.*

24

Chase

I REACHED PAST the thorns and picked a few more blueberries. I popped one in my mouth and the rest went into Jackie's saddle bags I had brought for toting them. At first, I had been nervous about eating the berries, but I was hungry. Plus, dying from poisonous berries sounded easier than dealing with Jackie, Harley, and Kinzie. I bit into the berry and relished the cool, wonderful juice. I'd been at it for almost forty-five minutes now.

Jackie and Harley were still chatting away—on what they talked about I had no clue, I tuned them out a while ago—but they didn't offer to help me, which I suspected. I didn't mind too much though. I was more focused on the blueberries. While those silly girls were yapping away, I was eating all the best berries. If I was the only one working, it seemed right that I should get the best. I was still gathering plenty for everyone else though. So far, I'd collected enough for all of us for two or three meals.

The bushes were packed with berries, and it didn't look like the ranch would run out anytime soon. I heard a few twigs snap and two horses nickered hello to one another. The first was Chance's familiar deep bellow and the other was less familiar, but still ingrained in my head nonetheless. It sounded like a song, one you'd heard only once or twice but still knew in your heart. I put a name to the sound a split second too late.

"Oh my gosh," Jackie whisper-shouted to Harley. "She's the most beautiful creature I've ever seen."

I jerked my head up and spotted the dappled-gray coat almost instantly. Raindancer stood ten feet from Chance. He was trying to go to her, and he would've succeeded if I had ground tied him like I usually did. Instead, I had tied him to a tree that stood alone, out in the open. He had seemed too spunky today, and now I knew why. Both horses were standing no more than forty-five feet from me, but even though they were so close, I couldn't see how Raindancer could be here. *How did she get inside the fence? She couldn't* be here.

My brain took too long to process what was happening. Jackie was quicker on her feet—um, horse. She and Harley spoke quietly and quickly under their breaths. They spread out to each side of Chance and Rain, easing past where I was at the end of the berry patch and closer to the other horses.

I had never messed with Jackie's stuff without permission, like when I unpacked for her today, or when I needed her saddlebags for the berries. I had asked, and she'd nodded without much thought. I still didn't go through her stuff though. However, I had seen her horse be tacked and untacked at least six times since we started this trail ride. So why, oh why, had I never noticed the *lasso* she had strapped under her canteen? She took it out deftly now, and Harley did the same with her own.

I had been thrilled when I learned that Jackie was an excellent roper. She may have been a pain to work with, but that skill was needed for the Horsemanship Olympics. But now, my heart tried frantically to claw itself out through my throat.

"Jackie, no," I meant to yell. I intended to get Jackie's attention and scare Rain off in the process. But my voice only came out in a hoarse, gasping whisper. Jackie clenched the lasso tighter in her hand, and her back stiffened noticeably. *She heard me. I know she did.* But she did not look back at me, did not make a move away from the mare, only closer. My lungs pulled in air in ragged breaths, and I dropped the bags full of berries. I shot up onto my feet.

Rain looked from the girls to me and then back to the girls. She did not know what they were planning. But when the girls crossed an invisible barrier, she did not dare to wait and find out. She bolted. Chance bellowed in confusion, but Harley and Jackie's horses knew what was about to happen a second before their riders spurred them into the chase. They were roping horses, herding horses, and they knew a job when they saw one. I let out a cry of anguish when the information came crashing on me. Jackie wanted to catch Rain, and it was my fault she saw her. For some reason, Rain came looking for me, or maybe Chance. But she was definitely here for one of us.

Chance's screech jarred me into action. I think he knew what was going to happen if we didn't do something. He jerked backward on the branch he was tied to. I was in motion now, going fast, but everything else seemed to speed up on me too. I reached Chance at the same moment as he wrenched himself free. As the reins flew in the air, I leaped at them. I seized them not a moment too soon, but the jolt I got from the momentum of Chance's pull almost made me fly into the air as well. My arm felt like it was being ripped free from my side. I ignored it. I swung onto Chance the fastest I ever had, and he charged forward as soon as I was halfway in the saddle.

Jackie and Harley were at least 300 yards away, and Rain was just forty or so feet in front of them. They were galloping at a tremendous speed, moving like machines. I thought of what Mrs. Karen said at the last barrel racing training session and prayed Chance was actually possible of it. I prayed he could *fly* for me in this moment.

Chance had always been one of my best friends. He was there to listen to me and to play with me. But today he was more than just a pet, he gave me his most powerful tool to control: his speed. Horses had to face a lot of dangers in the wild: mountain lions, fire, drought, and hundreds of other things. To survive, they had to be faster than the danger. You didn't see true, heartfelt, mustang speed unless that horse knew what it was like to run from these things. The ones who had this extra speed were the mustangs. The wild ones who could never be tamed. But today, Chance seemed to remember the life he almost lived, the life of a mustang.

Heat and sun and wind collided with my face at a torrential speed. We were gaining ground on the other horses. Chance was doing it; he was showing me he could fly. Trees began to rise up here and there in front of Rain. She dodged them at blinding speed. She ran almost like a shadow, or mist that stayed in the air for a minute then was gone forever.

As the trees rose up thicker and a forest began to form, Rain turned sharply to the left, running beside the trees, but refusing to go into them. The only way she would escape was if she outran her pursuers. *But how long could she keep this up?* She was not as fast as I imagined she would be. There was almost a hiccup in her gallop. She was not herself today. If she was, she would have pulled away from Jackie and Harley by now. Chance and I were about 200 yards away now. We turned as little as possible. We took the fastest route toward Rain, jumping over obstacles like stumps and fallen limbs if need be. *But it might not be enough.* Jackie and Harley weren't getting much closer to Rain, but Rain couldn't seem to pull away. She let out a cry. It almost seemed like a pained one, but not sorrowful pain. This cry was one of *actual* pain. *Her leg. It must still be hurt. But it couldn't be. It looked almost healed up the last time I saw her, and that had been almost two months ago.*

I would've slapped myself in the face if I thought I could've held onto Chance at the same time. *Some wounds were on the inside.* That log fell on her leg and smashed it into a rock. She must've bruised it *really* badly. *Could it have really healed by now? Was she still hurt? Or was it a fear of reinjury? Some people with old injuries said they experienced something called phantom pain. The wound might have been healed, but the mind was not.* She was still the fastest horse I had ever seen—sorry Chance—but I wasn't sure she had the stamina today.

The mare took us on a mad chase across hills, valleys, and made dozens of sharp turns to evade us. But Jackie and Harley kept up. Chance and I were a hundred yards behind them now. Jackie and Harley's voices were being flung into the wind, sharp and loud, but I couldn't decipher any of it. Even without being able to hear them, I knew they wouldn't stop unless forced. Which meant I was going to have to find a way to force them. But first, we had to catch them.

Chance was a force to be reckoned with. He was breathing hard, his coat soaked in sweat, but he never faltered or slowed down. If anything, he sped up. He seemed to know what was at stake here. He had lived his entire life in some cage or another. Sure, he had a wonderful home, but nothing compared to the wild plains. Rain had only ever known the outdoors, where nothing caged her. If she was caught, she would die. Maybe not physically, but she wouldn't have her heart anymore. She would stop living. Chance knew that, and so did I.

She probably didn't feel it yet, but she was surrounded. The camp was 700 acres after all. But it was fenced in. To escape, she'd have to get out the same way she got in, if she could remember how to do that.

We were now only a horse's length behind Harley and Jackie, who were riding about seven feet apart. In a couple more strides, we were parallel to them.

"Jackie," I screamed over the thundering of hooves. "You have to stop."

"Don't you see her?" Jackie hollered to me, pointing one hand forward. "She's incredible. I have to have her."

"You can't. She's not yours."

"She's not yours either." Jackie kicked harder into Sugarfoot's sides. The mare was lathered in sweat and foaming at the bit. Forget just stopping Jackie from hurting Rain, she was about to run her horse into the ground, and she didn't even see it. I reached out and grabbed onto Sugarfoot's reins, pulling back on them as I did the same thing to Chance.

"You're not going to have a horse at all if you keep this speed up much longer," I yelled at her. I hoped my voice was strong and clear and to the point. I hoped she got it. She *needed* to stop.

Jackie glanced at Harley who must've heard me. The other girl was already slowing her horse down. Jackie may have wanted to catch Rain, but Harley had enough sanity and care for her horse to slow her bay down. Harley's horse slowed at a rapid pace and came to a halting stop.

As I was letting a breath of relief out, I felt something bite into my skin, hard and sharp. I jerked my head around to my arm which was already red and throbbing. Jackie *whipped* me with her lasso. I automatically released my grip on Sugarfoot's reins and curled my arm up against my chest. Jackie kicked Sugarfoot hard, and she blazed back to the breakneck speed she was at before. My eyes were watering from the pain in my arm, but I couldn't let it stop me.

"Chance, we can't let—" I was cut off by him hurling himself with renewed energy at Jackie. We had to end this, *now*. We came thundering up to Jackie and pulled ahead of her a few feet, and then, without thinking, Chance and I collided into the other pair. The momentum that we both shared knocked the horses apart. Chance staggered and nearly collided with the ground. Nearly. By some miracle, he didn't fall, but stood, albeit shakily, with his head low and legs trembling. But at the same time, Sugarfoot was thrown back, and since Chance was bigger, the impact was worse for her.

She reared in terror and tried to catch herself but fell back instead. Jackie was flung to the side, so Sugarfoot didn't land on her. The mare was in shock, but managed to stagger to her feet, which meant nothing was broken, thank goodness. I quickly—as easily as I could—guided Chance over to Sugarfoot. I grabbed her reins and pulled her behind Chance and me before Jackie could get up.

"What in the world were you thinking, Hope? You could've killed me." *She's right. I could've killed her.* But I hadn't been thinking about that. I had been thinking about how I couldn't just do nothing. She had gone after Rain. *Had she considered the mare's safety? Or Sugarfoot's?*

"I wasn't going to let you hurt her," I said, deadly calm, quiet. I looked over to Rain who had stopped off in the distance. She was bone-tired and needed rest, but if we continued to chase, I was sure she would run. She would run until her heart burst. But right now, she drew in breaths and stood still, watching me.

I did not hear what Jackie was yelling. I did not know how long I sat there. But I stayed long enough for the mare to have a break. My eyes were now focused back on Jackie in case she made a move to her horse. Out of the corner of my eye, I saw Rain begin to trot away, looking back every now and then to make sure her pursuers had given up. I waited until she had been out of sight for ten minutes before turning Chance the opposite way, back the way we came. I could do nothing else for Rain right now but pray she found her way back outside the fence.

As we—Chance, Sugarfoot, and I—rode back, we went carefully. The horses needed to take it easy. We met up with Harley who wouldn't look me in the eyes. I didn't care. Just like I didn't care that Jackie was still whining, screaming, and yelling. I made her walk all the way back to the campsite on her own two feet.

25

Broken Truce

FOR THE NEXT day and a half, Jackie didn't talk to me. She just glared and scowled. We had moved to another campsite. This one was much like the first, woody and near a stream. We had fish and sandwiches and what was left of the blueberries. I had gone back for the bag of fruit when Jackie stopped talking to me. That didn't seem to make anything better except that Harley wasn't mad at me. The two other girls stayed around. We didn't worry about separating the phones or campsite anymore; I had lost the fight. I didn't like it, but the truce with Jackie had gone up in flames. She wasn't going to let me kick out her friend, and if I wasn't careful, I would be the one being kicked out.

I'd felt strange lately. Harley and Kinzie didn't hate me, but they treated me like I didn't exist. They didn't seem to care to allow me into their circle or space of thought. Jackie was purposefully ignoring me. It was actually impressive how good she was at avoiding anything that would bring me into the conversation.

But even with all the cold shoulder treatment, I continued to feel like I was being watched. *It couldn't be Rain, could it? No. She would be too smart to come near humans again.* My heart sunk. *She had been coming for me,* I thought. *Why else would she have come so far from where I first saw her? My house is what? Ninety miles from this ranch? And I saw her somewhere in the open lands near Kat's house, which is another ten or fifteen miles farther. Could she really have traveled all that way?* She must have, because I had seen her. My gut twisted into knots thinking about the brutal chase Jackie had started. *Who cares if she is furious with me?* The truce between Jackie and I had obviously been broken, but I'd do it again in a heartbeat.

My legs were pumping fast beneath me. I was galloping away, far away. That creature with two legs would never catch me. I would never let her. But I was tired, the adrenaline rush long gone. I slowed against my will, my exhausted body straining under the exertion. Usually, a run like that wouldn't have tired me so much. But the pressure on my left hind leg had aggravated the limb from the accident earlier in the season. It would be sore for days now.

I had come to a stop behind a few trees and bushes. I swung my long neck around to inspect the offending limb. To even see the bruising, I had to squint, but the inside was taking longer to heal than usual. We'd been moving the herd more. The mountainside we'd inhabited for most of the winter and spring was getting sparser and more barren. We'd needed to relocate for a little while, to somewhere with more food for the young foals who were born with spring, and the mares who had them. Because of the move, I had been out more. The herd couldn't travel as fast as a single horse could. So, for half of the day, The General and I got the herd a little farther toward lower ground, down closer to the water levels where the grasses would be growing well. That was where we were heading, to find a nice meadow and some woods to stay in for a while.

The second half of the day, I would scout ahead for the next leg of the trip. I had to make sure I didn't take the herd across hard terrain: no big rivers, steep gorges, or anything else that could prove treacherous for the new members of the herd. All of this traveling had kept my bruised leg from truly healing. I wouldn't let it show in front of the herd, especially not The General or Magma. Father would be worried about me taking on more responsibility that should go to a more mature mare. Magma would be overjoyed if I were to step down from the lead mare position. He would hate to have his sister be in charge with him which only made my heart hurt more. Magma wouldn't be a good leader. *But what is the better option? Let another stallion swoop in and take us all, or only take the mares and leave the foals? Never.*

I had allowed myself to rest for too long. I began walking again. My limp wasn't prominent; I didn't allow it to be. I made my way back to the herd. My journey was slow, but I didn't stop. I'd get back to the herd in time to bed down for the night. The trip back was quiet, which was nice. The only sounds were the squeaks and squawks of smaller woodland creatures.

I crossed a stream and went through a winding path with cliffs on one side. The groove cutting into the earth wasn't deep, just about ten feet or so, but the wall kept me protected from view on one side. When I was nearly back to where I left the herd, I passed several tree branches attached together in a row.

The General told foals the stories of the two-legged creations. One was a way to keep animals in one spot. They called it a fence, a cage. I couldn't believe I didn't see it on my way in. This part of the two-leg made wall was broken down, allowing about a fifteen-foot gap. I must have been so dazed this morning I didn't notice it. *I'll have to be more careful. The two-legs are closer than I thought. We'll have to go a different way tomorrow. I can't bring them past the wall, or we may get trapped. No wonder those two-legs saw me.*

I needed to get the herd farther away. But another part of me wanted to go back. I knew it was crazy of course, but I had seen the two-leg who had saved me, the one who had gotten the log off my leg. She had been kind and gentle and caring. I did not understand two-leg speech, but the look on the girl's face when her companions came at me was a look of horror. Then she had gotten on her horse like the other two-legs and given chase. But she hadn't been chasing me, she had been after her own kind. She had intentionally rammed herself and the horse she rode into the other two-leg to stop her.

Is it possible that the two-leg wants me free? Has she helped me yet again? And why? The General told stories of the two-legs, how they wanted to control everything they saw. They were evil. But the girl didn't seem like that. *Is she different, or does she have other motives for saving me?*

26

New Enemies

THAT NIGHT, DINNER was the usual: sandwiches. I hoped the Trail Trial didn't last much longer because I was tired of peanut butter and jelly. I could tell the others were too. This evening marked the fifth day of the trial. *How many teams are left?* It felt weird not knowing how many kids were still out there. *What if it is only us four left, and by Jackie hanging out with Harley we are actually all keeping each other in the game?* I wished we had a list of all the people who got out every day, so at least then we would know how much longer the game might last. After I thought this through, I realized it sounded too much like *The Hunger Games,* and that wasn't a good comparison. This was a fun game to get points. There was no killing involved. That might change though if I kept getting on Jackie's bad side.

We were almost done eating, and I was about to put out the fire when things got interesting. And by interesting, I mean downright terrifying. I saw the first one standing on a rock overlooking the area we had camped in. The five-foot vantage point may not have been much, but from where I was sitting, the angle made it look like the dog was a lot bigger than it really was.

Dog was the wrong word. His teeth were sharper than my knife by the looks of them. His fur might have been a light gray, but in the dark with the dirt and grime and the firelight, he looked like the dark color of death. Even with Jackie and the other girls talking and giggling in between me and the wolf, I still heard the snarl of a threat he was giving. *There aren't supposed to be wolves in Oklahoma anymore,* part of my brain thought. Another part thought that it didn't matter. *Wolf, coyote, or wild dog, it looks hungry and mean.*

"Girls, don't make any sudden moves," I said, reaching my hand out toward them. They looked up at me, surprised I had dared to speak. The glow of the fire on my face must've given me an urgent look, because only one of the three girls questioned me.

"You look absolutely terrified, Hope," Jackie said with a sneer. "What is it? Did you hear something creepy in the distance?" I did not look at her right away; my gaze focused on another predator that had come to the edge of the clearing. I spotted at least two more out of the corner of my eye. The horses began to notice we were surrounded. They nickered nervously to each other.

Dash did more than that. He pulled on his lead rope as hard as he could. The wolves may not have been necessarily large, but they were as big as him. They growled to each other; one of them barked. Then suddenly, everything happened. The girls shrieked. The horses reared up on their hindquarters or jumped to the side. Dash managed to pull his halter off his head. He bolted, and then the wolves gave chase.

I may have been scared of the wolves, but there was one thing that I was scared of more, and that was losing either of my horses. The wolves had all lunged after one of the weak links in our pack—not to say Dash was weak, he was just fun-sized—and left us alone. I was not about to leave Dash to the wolves. I bolted up and hurled myself in the direction of Chance. I had ridden him just a half hour ago to scope the perimeter, so he still had his bridle on. I had, however, already taken off all the other tack. It didn't matter though; I was pretty good without the saddle. Sure, I had never been chasing down wolves, but I had to ignore the part of me that thought I couldn't do it. Chance was prancing in his spot, shuffling from one side to another. His head was flung back, and the whites of his eyes were visibly showing.

"Easy, boy. It's going to be okay," I crooned, my arms stretched out in a pleading gesture. "We're going to help Dash." I didn't think he believed me, but at the mention of his little buddy, he stood still long enough for me to untie him and hoist myself onto his back. It seemed like he knew what was at stake.

"Hope, where are you going?" Kinzie screamed. I ignored her. The girls would have to worry about their horses and the other miniature pony. I was completely focused on rescuing Dash.

"Heeya," I screamed as I kicked Chance into a mad dash. He surged forward, automatically heading the direction the pack had went. The trees didn't seem to faze Chance. He dodged right and left efficiently. A few branches came close to me, but I dodged and ducked. It took us almost no time at all to catch up to the wolves. Or maybe it was just that time sped up around me.

Dash was only a few feet in front of the leader. He may have hated exercise, but he was like a bullet when it came to matters like this. As we were racing by, I was almost clobbered by a tree branch a little thinner than my arm but a few inches longer. I grabbed at it before it could hit me. The momentum almost wrenched my arm out of place, but instead the branch came loose. I had it in my hand not a moment too soon.

One of the wolves, the red color of dried blood, didn't like us interfering. He bared his fangs and leaped sideways at us. I swung the branch with all my might. My shoulder screamed in pain—and I might have screamed as well—but the blow made a solid connection to the beast's head. He was flung to the floor and clambered up wobbly. He shook his head back and forth to clear it. Once he got his senses back, he bolted, not in our direction but the other way, away from us. I had an idea.

"Aaaaaaahhhhh!" I bellowed at the top of my lungs. I swung Chance toward the nearest wolf. This one came at me much like the other one and also went down the same way. Another wolf came at us from behind. Chance kicked out at it with his hind legs when it got too close. The wolf sped away whimpering. The last two wolves were still intently chasing Dash.

I kicked Chance to speed him up. He tore through the woods at a faster pace, gaining on the wolves. When they noticed their buddies were nowhere to be seen and a large angry mass was on their tails, they forgot about Dash and split to the right. I urged Chance to get closer to Dash so we could slow him down.

The moon, which had been lighting our way thus far, suddenly flickered out. The trees were much denser here, which was probably why I didn't see the big tree branch bending over our path until my head slammed into it. I was flung off Chance, and for a moment, I felt like I was falling off a cliff. The smacking noise of my body against the tree limb was too much for the already frazzled horses. Chance didn't seem to realize he had lost his rider.

All of this went through my head in the time it took for me to be lifted off my horse and slam into my side on the ground. The pain came quickly, and darkness followed behind, pulling me deep into unconsciousness.

27

Bruised And Battered

THE INSTANT I regained consciousness, I wished the blackness would come and swallow me up again. Pain shot up my right leg and hip in a constant, merciless, pain. My shoulder throbbed. The added pounding of my head made all these things a hundred times worse. I pushed up with my good arm and hand, blinking several times, trying to figure out how long I had been lying on the ground.

I willed my eyes to adjust to the fading of the sunlight. *The fading of the sunlight. Is it getting dark again? I had been out here at least a day? And no one's found me?* My heart began to race even faster at the prospect of being hurt and alone, in the dark. It wasn't so bad last time because I wasn't conscious. But now, I was awake and freaking out. *There is no reason to be afraid of the dark, it can't hurt you,* I thought. I sucked in a deep, rattling breath. I had almost calmed myself down enough to think of a plan when a dark part of my mind replied, *but what about the creatures in the dark?*

My body shuddered profusely, and I grew more frightened for every inch the sun sank into the horizon. *Mom, Dad, I wish you were here. Everything hurts, and I don't know what to do.* Trees surrounded me on all sides, the shadows beside them grew and grew until I could not see any part that was not touched by them. I didn't know how long I sat there, paralyzed. It could have been hours or minutes. But it was long enough for it to become almost pitch black. The moon might have been out, but the trees blocked any chance of its reassuring glow.

I finally came partly to my senses. I did something that should've been my first reaction to this terrible turn of events. I prayed. *Dear God, oh . . . I'm so scared. I don't know what to do. But I know I need you. . . . Please, give me strength . . . and courage. Help me to figure this out. Give me your guidance.* I looked around again, and I realized something even more terrible than being on my own. *What happened to Chance and Dash? Where could they have gone? Were they hurt? No, don't think about that. They probably just got spooked and ran off a little way.*

"Chance? Dash?" I called out shakily. The trees gave the answer. They were dark, grim, and silent. "Chance? Dash?" I shouted this time. My voice shook, but I called out again, and again, and again. I was screaming now. I screamed as loud as I could. But they did not come. Neither of them heard me. I was alone. By the time I lost my voice, I was exhausted. My throat seemed to have swollen to twice its regular size. My heart pounded in my head as loud as if I had still been screaming. The pain in my leg and shoulder fought to be felt as well. It was too much to take, and the blackness consumed me once more.

There was something wet on my face. Someone was pressing a warm towel on my forehead to ease the pain. I sighed contentedly. But as I was soaking in its warmth, I realized it was not a rag on my forehead, and it was not water on the rag. My eyes shot open and swiveled back and forth to try and comprehend what I was seeing. I saw a large gray-and-white mass looming over me. It shifted like it was alive and quivered as it breathed. *Ghost.* Okay, I admit it wasn't the smartest conclusion to come to, but under the circumstances, I deserved a break.

As I began to focus and become more awake, my good old friend, pain, showed up again. It coursed through my veins and set my body on fire. Through the foggy haze my brain was trapped in, I saw the form that was truly standing over me. *Raindancer.* I surged up, my hands pushing me into a sitting position. The pain in my bad arm dulled slightly in my excitement.

The mare shied away, realizing I was conscious again. The magic that held her next to me vanished, and she was once again a wild horse, a creature who feared everything she didn't recognize or understand. A horse knew its most powerful tools were its hooves, capable of carrying them away from harm as fast as the wind. Raindancer was a regular horse in this matter, and I was stupid enough to think she wasn't.

"No, Rain, don't go!" I shouted. It was another mistake. Instead of comforting the mare into staying, my words merely shoved her farther away. She bolted away from me, heading for a large patch of bushes growing thick among the trees. It took her mere seconds to dart behind them and out of sight. From there, the only indication of her getting farther and farther away from me was the thumping of her hooves. It was only a few moments before I couldn't hear them anymore. The only thumping beat left came from my aching heart. I took no notice of the sun creeping higher into the sky—an indication that time was still moving like it always did—because my internal clock was broken, moving one minute and frozen in place the next.

The third time I woke up was much like the first two in that my body hurt more than it had ever hurt in my life. The sun was up. It was warm and cheerful and almost brightened my mood.

That was until I put weight on my right arm, and pain shot up to my shoulder. I used my left arm to push myself into a sitting position that didn't agitate my right leg too much and turned to look at my shoulder. I winced at the sight. My arm had turned a sickly shade of purple, black, and in some parts yellow, from my wrist to as far as I can see on my shoulder. Looking back now, grabbing the branch and swinging madly at the wolves was probably not the wisest choice. *But what else was I to do? Leave the horses to their deaths?* No. I didn't regret my choice.

I tried to assess the situation. I reached out and rolled up my right pant leg. It was cumbersome with just the one arm. The bruising was much the same as my shoulder. It might have been a bit better, but not much.

I didn't remember a lot about my glorious fall off the horse except that it hurt, a lot. *Had I fallen on a rock or landed on something hard imbedded in the ground or just ended up on top of some hard dirt?* Regardless, the landing had not been smooth, and I would have the bruising for months to tell the tale. I looked around for anything I might possess that would help me get out of this. I had jumped on Chance bareback last night—actually, it was the day before or maybe even the day before that—but whichever way it was, he had no saddle. This meant he didn't have the canteens on him or his saddle bags: no water, no food, no phone to contact help. I had nothing.

If Mom was here, she'd bring me something warm to eat, and my stomach wouldn't hurt so bad. If Dad was here, he'd make me laugh, help me to forget about the pain, and then carry me in his arms to safety. But all my wishing wouldn't bring them here. They didn't even know I was in trouble, probably no one did.

Tears pooled in my eyes. I clenched my hands together really tightly and took three long breaths in and out. I sent up a silent prayer, then looked around again. But this time, I wasn't looking for my things that weren't there. I was looking for something that *could* be there. There had to be water or food somewhere near here. The birds lived in the trees, so did the chipmunks and squirrels. At least one wild horse roamed these woods; Rain had been proof of that. The wolves lived close—hopefully not too close—and they had to have plenty of meat to eat, which meant even more animals lived here. All of this added up to one thing: there was food and water here.

Just as I thought I was out of luck, my eyes landed on something circular and bright red in the distance. I only saw it because the light bouncing off it caught my eye. I squinted. Hanging ten feet in the air was an apple. And if it was hanging in the air, it must be attached to a branch, which meant a whole apple tree. *Yes, food.* My stomach grumbled at the same moment. *How long had it been since I had something to eat? At least thirty-six hours, probably more.* But as I was thinking all of these things, I remembered one crucial fact, and that fact was attached to my hip. I might have been able to travel with a busted-up arm, but a leg too? The apple tree had to be at least two football fields away. Now would have been a good time to realize I was secretly MacGyver or something.

I focused on what was closest to the place I sat. About twenty feet off, a stick of wood about my height lay on the ground. I shifted myself a foot in its direction using my good leg and arm. My bad leg scraped across the brittle, dry dirt and white-hot pain burned the lower part of my leg. I whimpered, biting down on my lip to keep from crying. Crying would do me no good. I pulled my pant leg all the way down and tucked it under my boot sock to keep it from moving.

The next time I moved closer to the stick, the pain was more of a bearable throbbing. It took me ten of those throbbing minutes to finally reach the stick. I almost wanted to shout in joy. But the stick had been ten feet away. I needed to go hundreds more to get to the apple tree. I staggered awkwardly into a standing position. It took me several minutes to get into the least painful position for the trek. The stick offered enough structure to keep most of my weight off my right leg. But because I had to hold the stick on my right side to keep the pain of my leg at bay, my right shoulder had to suffer. The next hour of labor was full of pain and whimpering.

When I was closer, I saw a stream of water running a few feet from the base of the tree. The water looked clean, but the stream was a mere trickle, barely half a foot wide. It was a joy to see, however, because it meant I wouldn't have to travel again for water. *Thank you, God.* When I finally reached the tree, I crumpled to the ground in relief and exhaustion. I had tears brimming in my eyes, waiting to fall. I didn't know if they were from happiness or pain, probably too much of both.

I sat against the tree with my eyes closed for a while, resting. When my throat begged for water, I finally roused from my stupor. I shuffled over to the stream. I didn't have the filter with me, but unfiltered water was the least of my issues at the moment. Reaching out, I cupped my hands together to drink. The water was cool and smooth running down my throat. It was a pleasant change from the sandpaper feeling I had been having that day. I drank the dehydration away, taking slow, long sips.

When I had enough water for the time being, I turned to the next most pressing matter. My stomach was knotting itself up from lack of attention. The apples were ten feet above my head, but for a hungry enough person, nothing was preposterous. I made my way slowly over to the trunk of the tree.

Balancing mostly on my left leg and sparingly using my hurt arm to keep myself upright, I swung my stick at the branches overhead. One, two, three, four apples hit the ground. My back slid down the trunk to the ground and I feebly grabbed the apples there. I ate every bite out of every single one of them. With my stomach unknotting itself, I was able to fall into a fitful sleep.

28

Friend

I WOKE UP in what I assumed was the early morning hours of the next day. Sleep had energized me, but the position I slept in made my back sore and most of the right side of my body was stiff from lack of motion. I looked around, not sure if I wanted to awaken my limbs yet. The pain in my side had diminished greatly, but I thought that was just because my body thought I was still asleep.

As I looked around, I noticed something moving behind a bush about thirty feet away. For some reason, I was not scared. Perhaps it was because a rustling sound in the early morning with bird sounds calmed instead of frightened me. Whatever the reason, I sat and watched the creature shuffle on the other side of the bush. I caught a glimpse of gray hair for a split second. Then a familiar whinny fluttered to my ears.

I had been staring closer to the ground, expecting the rustling to be coming from a rabbit or some other woodland creature. When I heard the noise of a much larger animal, my eyes shot up to the top of the bush where a large head was poking out. The creature stared at me with eyes so much wiser and stronger than a bunny's. Dark eyes stared into my hazel ones.

"Rain." My voice broke when I said her name. It was the first actual word I had spoken since the night I screamed myself to sleep calling for Dash and Chance. *She can't be here again. Didn't she find her way back to freedom?* I shook my head. It was a hallucination, nothing more. I looked back up, and Rain was gone, no longer behind the bush. But when I looked around for her, I actually saw her again. She had not run off. This time, she stood a few steps to the right and closer to me. She was not looking at me directly anymore, but above me. She took a few more steps, and I held my breath, unwilling to frighten her off again for something as trivial as breathing.

Her head swung down to be level with mine as she contemplated my presence. Her head moved back up to look at the apples. She continued to walk forward until she was ten feet away. Rearing up on her hind legs, she snagged an apple from the tree. The jerk of the branch made another apple fall, but this one almost fell in my lap. I grabbed onto it, and clutched it tightly in my hand, willing myself not to wake up if this was a dream.

Raindancer ate the apple with relish and only looked at me when she was done with it. She regarded me calmly. When I could hold my breath no longer, I let it out. She didn't seem bothered by my presence. I was on the ground and had hurt two of my limbs. She seemed to know that and was unconcerned with being chased.

She stayed close for a couple of hours, pretending to ignore me and focus on eating grass. Still, I could tell there was a chance I intrigued her. While she was busy eating, I talked to her softly.

"You wouldn't happen to know where Chance and Dash are, would you?" She flicked her ears toward my voice, but other than that she made no sign she'd heard me. "Chance is the horse I was riding the first time we met." I did not mention the chase. Horses were smart animals. I didn't want her connecting the chase to me. "You haven't met Dash though. He's about this high." I held my left hand up and waved it gently at the height I was describing. "Short little guy, but he can eat as much as any horse three times his size."

I let out a sad chuckle. Rain made no indication she knew who these horses were, but I didn't really expect her to. "Well, if you see them, tell those goofballs they forgot the last member of their herd, the one that feeds them and brings them sugar cubes." This time she nickered in reply. Maybe "herd" was a word she understood.

This creature was a real puzzle. She talked in a language I did not understand, with more noises and less gestures. Horses communicated mostly in body language, but this two-leg seemed to use mostly noise from its mouth to talk. I did not pretend I knew what she was saying, and I think she got that. She kept making a noise over and over when she wanted to get my attention: Raindancer. It seemed the creature had named me. I did not know how to tell the weird creature my name was Skytears.

I was named after the water that fell from the sky, the water that brought nourishment to the valleys, a force that could be gentle and powerful. But maybe, Raindancer was the two-leg's name for Skytears. I did not name the two-leg like she did me, but I did grow rather attached to her. When I left her later that afternoon to go check on the herd I had safely tucked away in a luscious valley, she seemed saddened. I called out to her in a way I hoped she could understand. *I will be back.* I did not know why I told her so. She didn't speak my language, and I shouldn't even be in the vicinity of her kind. But with her sitting there alone and hurt, with no one to keep her company, my heart ached. She didn't seem bad, and she saved me from the others of her kind. The least I could do was keep her company a little, until her herd came back for her.

29

Sneaking Out

I GALLOPED THROUGH an open stretch of land, completely infuriated with my father. After only two mornings of being gone from the herd, my father was growing anxious about me. Magma just had to point out the fact that I went off on my own a lot. Father immediately tried to get me to stop. He was worried other stallions might try to steal me away. True, if I was caught that would be a horrible turn of events. But I hadn't met a horse faster than me except for *him*. I didn't dare let myself think too much on the fact that my friend was gone. But the truth still remained: I was fast enough to stay out of the reach of any stallion who tried to take me and smart enough to sneak out of the valley without any of the herd noticing.

I was on my way to meet the two-leg again. She was such an odd thing I couldn't help but like her. I knew the way well now and wasn't paying much attention because I was still pretty mad about the way my father had treated me. *He acts like I am still a filly. After weeks of traveling and guiding the herd, he thinks it isn't safe for me to venture out on my own for a few hours? The nerve.* I was so busy thinking this I didn't notice the horse blocking my path.

The big paint stood with his neck arched and stomped his front hoof into the dirt three times. I supposed he was going for a commandingly handsome look. It wasn't working. To me, his posture just screamed *hey, how about we run off together, and I become your master for all eternity. It'll be great.* I was not impressed. I moved to go around him, but he blocked me.

I puffed out a breath and glared at him. *Back off. I have somewhere to be.*

"My name's Paco," the paint whinnied. "You're not from around here, are you? I haven't seen you before. I could show you around if you want." He made no move to get out of my way. His tone didn't match his friendly questioning, and he seemed like a stallion who resorted to brute strength more often than necessary.

"I'm fine on my own, thank you," I whinnied back. I made another move to go around him, but he blocked me.

We did not speak with our voices anymore. We used a flick of our ears or a swing of our neck and head. We used our hoof beats. His message was clear. *You are staying with me.* But mine was also clear. *Not if I have anything to say about it.*

My hooves jolted into motion, propelling me backwards. Paco fell for the trick and barreled toward me. While he was charging at me, I shot off to the right and used my legs for what they were good at: running. Paco surprised me with a powerful set of hindquarters. He was fast, but with all that muscle to carry, he'd get tired a lot faster than I would, at least if my leg held up. Every time I thought I had gotten better, some freak-show came in and started chasing me.

Paco did not give up the chase easily. After about seven minutes, he was still hot on my tail. *Wow, this guy is desperate.* I thought he was beginning to slow down. But just as I thought that, a shadow plowed in between Paco and me. Paco's hooves dug into the ground, sinking deep into the earth to stop himself before he ran into the other horse. He managed to stop, but not at all gracefully.

Usually, I would continue running and be happy about my luck, but I was too confused by Paco's sudden halt. I swung around and came to a halt, gazing back at where Paco stood stock-still. Another horse stood in front of him, neck arched in a way that clearly said the chase was over, at least for him.

The newcomer was a stallion with a coat colored the same shade of the darkest night I had ever seen. He stamped his foot and took a few steps closer to Paco. When the paint didn't comprehend the command, the black was more forceful. He reared up on his hind legs so close to Paco he had to move or else be clobbered by the black's thundering hooves. Paco, for all his brawn, had no bravery when it came to fighting other stallions. He ran.

From what I could see, the black didn't have more muscle. He might've been faster, but this close, muscle was more important than speed. Still, maybe I was missing something. Too late, I realized I had been saved from one stallion by another. This one was probably no better than the last. Before I had time to bolt, the black stallion turned and looked me right in the eyes.

30

Reunion

IN THE BLINK of an eye, literally, the stallion's face changed from rage to shock and then to excitement. I took a few steps back, almost tripping over my own legs. This stallion was different from Paco. I could see it in his eyes. *He's smart.* The way he blazed in here was proof of his speed. I wasn't sure if I could outrun him if I tried.

"Look, I'm really grateful for the assist, but I didn't need help," I neighed. My rising panic made my tone ruder than I intended. The stallion's eyes flew open in recognition, as wide as they could go.

"Skytears?" His neigh was deep and warm. He skipped a few steps closer to peer at me intently.

I shook my head in confusion and leaned away from him. *How do you know my name?* I backed away as many feet as he took forward. I hated to seem like a scared filly, but he might turn out to be more than I could handle. *How could someone I have never met, someone who came out of nowhere, know my name?* But even as I thought this, I got a better look at the horse in front of me. His eyes were so familiar, like I was looking at myself reflected in a pool. He carried himself like someone who didn't think he had strength. In the twitch of his ears and the shuffle of his feet, he reminded me of someone I thought was dead.

"Fleetfoot?" I whinnied quietly, not daring to hope it was true. But it had to be. He was standing right in front of me.

He smiled and pranced toward me. *You're alive.* I let out a high-pitched neigh of excitement. I bounded toward him, and he did the same. When we came together, neither of us could stand still. We leaped around each other.

"I can't believe it," Fleetfoot neighed. "After all this time, I thought I would never see you again."

"Thought? I knew I wouldn't see you again. We all thought you were dead." But in my excitement, there was another emotion: anger. I rammed my shoulder into him. "Where have you been?"

"It's a long story."

"Why didn't you come back?"

"Also, a long story."

I would have sat down like a coyote if that was comfortably possible. Instead, I planted my hooves and looked at him pointedly. *I've got time.*

Hours later, we were still catching up on everything that had happened to us since the split up. While I had grown up in the herd and become the boss mare, Fleetfoot had been captured. Directly after the earthshake that we thought killed him, a group of two-legs found him and tried to train him to do their bidding. It took him nearly a year to get loose, and when he did, he had no idea where he was. The two-legs took him far away from anywhere he recognized.

Since then, he had struck out on his own. He found a band of loners he stayed with for a while but eventually left. He tried to start his own band, but he wasn't strong enough to fight the stallions for the mares who wanted a different leader. Funny how that worked. The strong ones were the bullies who could get away with it. The stallions he could beat were nice and the mares didn't want to leave, and Fleetfoot was too nice to take them. My friend had been through a lot in the past year and a half. It was only after a little while that I came to my senses.

"Come join our herd again," I neighed gleefully. It was all I'd ever wanted. This would solve all the problems with the herd.

"I can't do that," Fleetfoot whinnied dejectedly.

"Why not?"

"Last time I checked," he began, "stallions don't let other stallions into their herds."

"The General is getting too old. He wants a successor so the herd doesn't go to some strange scumbag who would hurt the foals. He would welcome you back."

"He already has a successor." Fleetfoot blew out a puff of air and shook his mane. *He means Magma. He doesn't think he could take on Magma.* Fleetfoot dug in the dirt with his hoof, and I almost didn't catch what he whinnied under his breath. "The herd would probably thank me if I was strong enough to kick him out."

I didn't say anything to make him think differently. We both knew it was true. We walked in silence for a while. I vaguely knew where we were at, but Fleetfoot seemed to be leading like this was his home.

How long have you lived here? I thought.

His answer was almost immediate, like he could sense my question. "A couple of months. It's been pretty peaceful. Not many of the other herds live this close to the two-legs because it would be dangerous. But I can get around pretty fast by myself. It's kind of nice not having to fight for land, but it does get lonely."

I bumped his shoulder gently, showing him how I felt without voicing it. *I can imagine.* As we trotted along farther into land I was not familiar with, I asked him, "Where are you taking me?"

"To my home," he whinnied. "Well, for now, at least." I tried not to hear the hopefulness in his voice. *Did he mean to say he would move if I left with the herd? Would he follow me?* I tried not to hope for the impossible.

I was pulled out of my thoughts when Fleetfoot said, "I've got some horses I want you to meet. They've been staying with me for the past couple of days until they find their friend."

Their friend? I wondered, confused. *Fleetfoot has other lone stallions staying with him?* It seemed unlikely that a couple of mares were out on their own. I was the only mare I knew of who wandered off on my own, but I'd rather meet a few mares over stallions any day.

We finally arrived at the place Fleetfoot called home. It was a sparsely wooded area at the base of a large hill with a cave imbedded in the side of it. I wasn't sure how far the cave went in, but it was definitely tall enough for a horse to stand in with their head all the way up. There was a three-foot-wide stream running across the entrance to the cave that must've been handy for midnight-dry throats. Fleetfoot nickered a greeting, and two voices echoed from the cave.

The speakers emerged a moment later. One was a stallion about my height with a bright coppery-colored coat and dark black stockings, mane and tail. The other was a fuzzy ball of black adorableness. This colt was a bit chunkier than most foals were at his age. His mother must just have fed him well. *Maybe that's who they are looking for?*

The stallion—whom I assumed was the father of the foal—whinnied, "Who is this, Fleetfoot?" His accent was a little different than what I was used to, but I wasn't sure what made it so.

"This is Skytears," Fleetfoot replied brightly. "She's an old friend I lost track of for a while. I only found her today." The stallion nodded in understanding but didn't seem to catch Fleetfoot's excitement. He looked glum and dejected.

"Fleetfoot told me you're missing a friend," I neighed. "Is she your mare—this foal's mother—who you're missing?"

"Foal. Who are you calling a foal? I'm old enough to be *his* father." The little horse neighed for the first time. His voice was high-pitched like a foal's, but most young horses couldn't form coherent sentences like that this early. I was astounded.

I gave him a quizzical look. "You're a stallion? Did you never go through a growth spurt?" I leaned my head in closer to him, so we were eye level. "Did you eat the weeds your mother told you not to?"

"Have you been hit in the head?" the little black stallion nickered. "No, I didn't eat weeds. This is just how I am. I'm a miniature pony—a Shetland. It's one of the characteristics of my breed. We don't get very tall," he paused for a moment and then added, "and my name's Dash. So, don't call me *foal* again."

"Don't mind him. He's just a little grumpy because he hasn't gotten a good brushing in a while," the buckskin explained. "My name's Chance." He shifted closer, and the light made something beside him flash. I took a closer look and realized it was on him. And it was *two-leg* made.

He was captured by two-legs. I backed away quickly, my legs shaking against my will.

"What?"

"They've strapped a controlling device on your head."

"Oh, you mean my bridle?" he asked, looking oddly calm about the whole situation. If I had a two-leg made thing anywhere *near* me, I would not be calm about it. "It's alright. It doesn't bother me much. Well, except for the fact that it's been stuck on my head for nearly a week. Hope usually takes it off at the end of the day, but since she's missing, I've had to wear it constantly."

"The person they're missing is a two-leg," Fleetfoot explained.

I shot him a look that said I'd picked up on that *tiny* detail. *Thanks, Captain Obvious.* "Wait," I had to backtrack for a second. "Did you say the two-leg was called Hope?" *The two-leg I've been seeing calls herself the same thing, doesn't she? Could this be the same girl they are looking for?*

"They call themselves humans. But yes, our girl's name is Hope," Dash answered for Chance.

"Does she have a blonde mane and hazel eyes?"

"Yes, how did you know?" Chance perked up, eager to hear my answer. Dash looked much the same. They both leaned toward me.

"Because I've met her," I answered.

I explained everything to them. I told them about meeting Hope and how she was. I told them I had seen her several times in the past few days and that she couldn't walk properly, and her arm—that's what Chance said a two-leg front leg was called—and head were bloodied and bruised.

"I was actually going to see her again when I ran into Fleetfoot."

"I'm going with you," Dash neighed promptly. "Hope needs me."

"I'm coming too," Chance agreed. "I need to make sure she's safe."

"That might not be the best idea," Fleetfoot whinnied.

"And why not?" Dash asked angrily.

"Hope is on two-leg, excuse me, human land, right?" His question was directed at me. I nodded. "Both of you are obviously owned by humans." He added this last part looking at the two stallions in front of me.

I could see what Fleetfoot meant. Though their coats hadn't been touched by a two-leg in several days, it was obvious that the two horses were fed, groomed, and taken care. Their coats were a little dusty, but they were smooth and their manes and tails had no knots in them. Their hooves were short and smooth. Any two-leg would see the obvious.

They were tame. Two-legs would try to catch them before they got to their two-leg. Fleetfoot made a good point, I had to admit.

"I would go, but I have no idea where this girl is," Fleetfoot whinnied and blew air out of his nose in reluctance, "which means the only option is you, Skytears."

"I can do it," I neighed confidently. "I haven't been caught yet. And believe me, I've had some close calls. Don't ask." I looked over in time to see that Chance had his eyes scrunched up in concentration. His eyes shot open moments later, and he blinked several times in rapid succession like he couldn't believe what he was seeing.

"You're Raindancer," he realized. "Hope helped you get your hind leg out from under the tree limb. She also tried to stop those other human girls from chasing you." He shook his head. "I've seen you four times now, and Hope talks about you all the time. I can't believe I didn't recognize you immediately."

I shook my head at my own stupidity. I hadn't recognized him either at first. But to be fair, I had been preoccupied with other things on all our encounters: tree limbs, the herd, and those crazy two-legs trying to catch me.

"But back to the matter of getting Hope safely home," Chance nickered. "I don't like the idea of just waiting here and letting you get her."

"I don't like it any more than you do, but Fleetfoot's right, you two are way too noticeable," I neighed. Chance huffed. "I'll get her here," I continued. "You guys figure out what to do next." I emphasized the last part so they would clearly understand what I meant. *I'll stick my neck out once for the two-leg who helped me, but just this once.* I left the stallions in the woods to make a plan. Me, I was working on a plan to keep this a secret from my father.

31

Assistance

I WAS NOT sure exactly how long it took me to get to the clearing where Hope was marooned. My brain felt like it was running ten times as fast as usual while my heart slowed to a crawl of something on the brink of death. It was a strange feeling: doing something I'd always been taught was dangerous but doing it anyway because it seemed the only possible solution. *Is The General right? Are all two-legs to be avoided because they are all the same—a cruel creature that only cares about itself?* I hoped he was wrong. Because if he wasn't, I was headed into a trap.

I opened my eyes when I couldn't take the darkness and pain anymore. My back was sore, and the tree I had been leaning up against had left indentions in my skin from prolonged contact with the tree bark. The pain gained in magnitude when I moved, but after stretching for a few minutes, it felt much better. I tried to concentrate on my back, and the ache in it. Everything in my body hurt, but my back was the least of those worries.

Maybe if I only think of my back, my swollen arm and shoulder will stop aching so bad. Maybe my right leg will miraculously heal so that I can walk. But maybes weren't going to get me out of here. *I have to get back to camp. I have to. But how? Start with something you can control, Hope.* I tried to swallow down my fear and pain, but it got stuck in my throat. I tried again, but it still wouldn't work. My mouth was too dry, my throat too scratchy. I needed water. That was something I could do.

I shifted my weight onto my left side, holding myself up with my arm. Using the wiggling motion I had been doing since my injury, I made my way to the tiny stream a few feet away. My arm burned by the time I got there. It may not have been a far distance away, and I had been having to do this for a few days, but my left arm was not dominant. My right arm was, and now my left arm had to be trained to do everything both arms usually did together.

I was too tired to cup the water and drink from my hands, so I just lapped at the water like a horse. I leaned back up when I was finished and took in a single breath that made me feel like everything would be alright. My stomach reminded me of another problem I had to fix; I was hungry. I looked up at the tree limbs behind me. They seemed so far away. My weary body ached even more when I thought about having to climb up the tree to get more apples. For the past few days, I had used a stick as a club to get the apples down. But now, the only apples left on the tree were the ones I couldn't even reach with the stick. I leaned back toward the water and drank some more, willing my body to be full so I wasn't hungry anymore.

I heard a twig snap, and my head jerked up. I didn't want something else to go wrong. My heart rate skyrocketed in the brief moment it took for me to focus on what was in front of me.

"Raindancer," I choked out. My throat was still raspy from screaming for Chance and Dash a few days ago, but I hoped Rain could hear the relief in my voice. I might have gone insane if it weren't for her these last few days. *Thank you, God, for putting her in my life. I don't know if I would have survived otherwise.*

I told Rain about what had happened since she had been gone. It was not much, considering I had hardly moved since she left yesterday. I dramatized the squirrels that had been in the woods last night and even gave them names to make them seem like they were my friends. I told her of the deer I saw sneaking around in the corner of my vision. I tried to make the story last as long as possible, because maybe I could get Rain to stay this time.

Though she seemed to have grown accustomed to my presence lately, today she seemed more skittish than usual. I looked up into a bird nest as I told her about the mother and babies that lived there. I didn't want Rain to feel uncomfortable with me watching her all the time. My ears picked up on the sound of her coming closer, bit by bit. When my story got to the part about a skunk that had come to speak with the squirrels, I heard water sloshing by the interruption of a hoof.

I glanced down at the two hooves now standing in the stream a foot away from me. My gaze traveled ever so slowly up to a strong chest, long graceful neck, and then to the eyes of my companion. She was looking at me like she couldn't quite figure out what to think of me. I held my breath, not daring to move a muscle and scare her away. *The only other time she got this close, I was unconscious. Well, that and the time she was the one with a hurt leg.* But last time, as soon as I had awakened, she bolted. I didn't want this time to be the same.

We stayed that way for a long time. She was contemplating something. I could tell by the look in her eyes. Horses have always seemed so incredible to me. Not only did they have strong legs to carry them wherever they wanted, but they had these big dark eyes that seemed to see things so much differently than I did. *I wonder what she thinks of me. Am I an oddity to her? Something to be feared? Or am I more of a nuisance to her kind?* I wished I could read her mind.

This two-leg was a strange creature. She crawled on the ground in pain but didn't get anywhere. She seemed calm for someone who had been abandoned by her kind. She talked a lot too, probably too much. *Doesn't she know I can't understand her?* Whenever I was with other wild horses, I believed what we had always been told: two-legs were too dangerous to be around. I almost had myself convinced, until I saw Hope again. She didn't seem so bad, but I had to be cautious. She might not intentionally hurt me, but many others of her kind would. Much like the two-legs who chased me until my legs throbbed, their kind could not be trusted.

I hoped this girl was the exception. I walked up toward her through the trees when her back was turned. I did not want to frighten her too much, so I stepped on a twig a few yards away from her. She whipped her head around, and her eyes landed on me. They widened, and then she froze, like she had just thought of something terrible. She began to breathe in quick breaths and started chattering about things that happened to her.

I didn't understand the noises coming from her mouth, though I tried to pick up on the meaning by reading her body language. The noises she made fell and rose as she looked around her, gesturing to the squirrels and birds in the trees. I caught the fear in her posture and voice. She was lonelier than she was letting on. I just stood there and watched her for a while. She didn't seem to mind. I was comforting her by just being there.

Two-legs seemed to be much like horses in that they didn't usually like to be alone. They had a family or group of two-legs they loved to be around, their herd. They felt safe, protected. *I wonder how I would handle being separated and hurt for so long, stranded where my herd could not find me. This two-leg is in a similar situation to when I hurt my leg. But this is much worse.* I think it was that thought that moved me to finally approach her. *I'll get her back to her herd.*

The mare blinked twice, then snorted, like she had made up her mind about something. She turned to the right, so I could see her side and then looked at me. *She wants you to ride her,* I thought. And then I nearly slapped myself. *Of course, that's not what she wants.* It was a stupid thought. But she stood there and watched me, like she was waiting on something. *Get up. She needs to take you somewhere.* I didn't know if the thought came straight from the Lord and was meant as a signal or if it was my tired brain overthinking the mare's posture, but I asked, "Do you want me to ride you?"

She nickered, and I interpreted it to mean she said "obviously." At least, I hoped that was what she meant.

Deciding to mount a wild horse with two injured limbs and nothing to help me get up was harder than it sounded. And it sounded hard. I struggled to my feet and placed my right hand on Rain's back. Her skin shuddered like the ruffling of a curtain beneath my touch. To get up on her, I would need to use both my legs. I groaned when I put weight on my right leg. Though I had not been on it for more than two days, it still sent fire up my body at any pressure. I gritted my teeth to stop myself from whimpering.

Rain was barely standing still as it was. She shuffled her hooves nervously, splashing water on my feet. I ignored the wetness in my toes and focused on the task at hand as best as possible. When she seemed to settle down a little, I stroked her gently and crooned to her.

Before I could talk myself out of it, I grabbed ahold of her mane and jumped up with my good leg. I tried swinging my right leg up but let a cry of pain slip out. Rain bounced to the side, jerking my hold free and depositing me in the stream. I might have cried; I wasn't sure. The water from the stream splashed on my face, but the water also tasted salty. Were the tears from the pain in my leg or the fact that Rain bolted? She was scared of me, and I was foolish to think this would be like the movies where the horse saved the girl. I pulled my good leg up to my stomach and wrapped my good arm around it. I rested my head on my arm and truly began to cry.

I didn't mean to do it, but I couldn't help myself. I finally thought I would make it back to Cowboy Camp, to my family. I had thought I would get better, I would find Chance and Dash, and I would be okay again. But I guessed that was not going to happen. As I cried and tried to accept my fate, I heard something I was sure I imagined.

I heard the clacking of pebbles and the sloshing of water being moved suddenly. The thud of a heavy animal's body hitting the ground followed a moment after. The water splashed me again, and I wiped the tears and stream water from my face. Through my bleary eyes, I saw Rain staring me down. She had laid down beside me and was looking at me again with the look that said she was waiting. But this time, her face seemed to say, "Get up. This is the last chance I can afford to give you." I struggled up onto my knees as carefully and calmly as I could.

What happened next, I must have dreamed. But in my sleep, I always had a dream or a nightmare. This seemed to be a mix of both. The fact that I was riding on the back of a wild horse out in unfamiliar woods was dreamlike. It was something my overactive imagination had done to me several times. But in those dreams, I never had a busted leg and shoulder. The pain was worse than any nightmare I could conjure up. It wasn't a foggy, dreary pain, like in most nightmares. It was sharp and harsh. It was the only reason I knew I wasn't dreaming.

Rain carried me farther into the woods and past a few valleys. I tried to keep up with where we were going. We passed another stream, one that could pass as a small river. Most landmarks I didn't recognize and soon was completely lost. Every step Rain took sent a jolt up the right side of my body, hitting my leg first and then moving to my shoulder. She must've noticed my whimpering because she slowed her trot into a swift walk. It helped a little, but the only thing that really helped was thinking that Rain knew what she was doing, and she was taking me to help.

After a bit, we came up on a fence line with several pieces on the ground. This must have been how Raindancer was able to get in and out of the camp's boundary line. I didn't know where she was taking me, but I continued to trust she could help me. I remained quiet as we left the fence behind us.

My sense of time must have been completely off, and I blamed my injuries for that. It seemed in the past few days, I couldn't tell the passing of time. After a while, Rain stopped our traveling. We were in a sparsely wooded area settled at the base of a large hill with a cave imbedded in the side of it. The cave was tall enough for a horse to stand with its head all the way up. A three-foot-wide stream ran across the entrance.

Rain lifted her head high and called out to whatever was in the cave. A clacking sound resonated from the cave, and three horses appeared. One was a little taller than my waist and dark ebony, the second was a buckskin with almost black stockings, and the third was a shadow of a horse. The color of night seemed fused into his coat. When the first two stepped fully out of the cave and the light hit them, I recognized the horses in front of me.

"Chance, Dash," I croaked. It came out louder than I expected, and Rain shied beneath me. I struggled to keep my balance and only barely managed. "Easy, girl. I'm sorry, I was only excited. Easy, girl. . . ." I reached my hand out and stroked her neck instinctively. She moved underneath me more when I did that. It was a stupid thing for me to do. A horse born and raised in the wild would not find comfort in the touch of a human.

I focused on touching her as little as possible. She seemed to calm down slightly when the dark horse nickered to her. The horse did not come closer but watched us intently. I looked back to where Chance and Dash were when I thought Rain had calmed down a bit. It took me a moment to find Dash. He had quickly reached my side, and I only noticed he was so close when he nipped my foot. Thankfully, it was my left, and was in semiperfect condition. He looked at me and then looked around at his surroundings in what could only have been disgust. He looked at me again as if to say,

"You've got to get me out of here, Hope. I don't belong in this uncivilized land."

I strained to keep the chuckle inside so I wouldn't scare Rain worse. I glanced up at Chance and was surprised to see how calm and at home he looked. He seemed happy to see me, but he also appeared completely happy in the meadow by the cave. I didn't have time to think much on what that meant because Rain began to shift and move under me. She stomped her front hoof in a clear message. *Get off.*

I knew I shouldn't push my luck too much. Rain had already done so much for me. It was time for it to come to an end though. Going slowly and trying not to whimper too much, I slid–fell off the mare. I had barely gotten my footing when Rain bolted over to the black horse. I took a closer look and almost passed out. The black horse wasn't a calm mare that was a little scared of me like I had thought in the beginning. He was a stallion, and the look on his face said he was looking for one sign to tell him I was a threat and should be terminated. *Is this Rain's stallion? He isn't Spirit, the stallion Chance and I met nearly three months ago. Why are Chance and Dash allowed in the presence of another stallion's herd?*

Dash seemed to be oblivious to the possible danger he was in. Or maybe the stallion didn't care since Dash was kind of a midget compared to him. Chance, on the other hand, was full-grown, and Spirit had hated the fact that Chance had even come close to the band of wild horses a few months ago. That brought up another good question.

Where are Spirit and the herd? The closest I could figure was that this black stallion had stolen Rain. If Rain was the first mare in the group, the black might have let Chance and Dash stick around as a sort of temporary bachelor herd. I had read about those once before. Sometimes, several young stallions traveled in groups for a while if they didn't have a herd of their own.

Dash rubbed up against me insistently and brought me out of my thoughts. Time to focus on the matter at hand. Chance still had his bridle on from when we went after Dash and the wolves. *I could ride back to the camp.* I was a little lost, but I refused to worry about that right now. In my experience, Chance usually had a better sense of direction than I did. I had other things to worry about, like hauling myself up onto another horse. I reached out my hand and stroked Dash to calm him down. With my other hand, I reached out and clucked softly to Chance.

"Come here, boy," I crooned. "I'm hurt, buddy, and you're the only one who can carry me." It took him too long to respond. He just stood there, like he didn't know me. "Come here, boy, please," I continued. "Let's get home."

This time, he showed that he heard me by flicking his ears toward me, but he still didn't approach. Tears pricked my eyes. Chance had always been like a puppy to me. We were best friends. *So why does this feel like he has grown apart from me?* He didn't act like a puppy anymore. He acted like a stray dog, one that didn't recognize me. The tears were pooling in my eyes now, and it wouldn't be long before I would break. My whole body had been hurting for days, the pain only ebbing when I slept. But the pain of the past few days was nothing like this. Chance had wild roots, and now he had gotten a taste of it. He liked the grass on the other side of the fence. *Chance doesn't want to go back to captivity. He wants to remain wild.*

32

Goodbye

I BEGAN TO freely cry. I knew I could scare Rain and Pitch with my sobbing—Pitch sounded like a cool name for a horse with his black coat. I tried to stop, but the tears came relentlessly. My heart wanted to curl into a pit and die. I willed myself to focus on Chance. Though he had been in the wild for a few days and not been taken care of like he was used to, he seemed healthier than ever. I knew he wouldn't look scrawny from only a few days out on his own, but something was different, maybe in the way he carried himself. He looked at home here, not like he had when he was in a pasture. There was an extra layer of belonging. I hated it. If he had looked sad but wanted to stay, or if I could think of a single reason why he wouldn't thrive here, it wouldn't have been this difficult.

I thought of the storms he would have to endure and the wild animals he would constantly have to look out for. He couldn't start a herd of his own as a gelding. *How would he survive?* But the way he held himself now told me he could handle himself and wanted to. So, I limped forward. He waited for me. He didn't shy away when I reached my hand out, he just looked straight into my eyes and straight to my heart. He told me with his eyes that this was what he really wanted, that he would be okay, that he would be happier than he'd ever been. I stroked his face for a moment and then, I took the bridle off.

I was crying more than I'd ever cried in my entire life. I leaned against Dash as he plodded forward. It was a good thing his legs were short because my body couldn't take a faster pace. We were half a mile away or so now. I let Dash lead the way. If anyone knew how to get home, it was Dash. My injuries were burning but I couldn't stop and rest. If I did, I was doubtful I'd be able to get back up again. Dash grunted and whinnied like he was giving me a rundown of everything that had happened in the past few days.

"I had to sleep in a creepy, wet cave. The food was terrible. I had to go get the grass all by myself. The other horses think they're better than me because they're taller." He seemed especially disgruntled by this last fact. Dash was many things, but he might have been too adorable for his own good. At the ranch, he was always smothered by little girls and boys vying for his attention, which he loved. It didn't seem the same held true for wild horses. *God, thank you for Dash. It means a lot that he loves home as much as me. I don't know what I would've done if both of my boys. . . . No. I can't think about that.* I closed my eyes to shut off the tears.

I squeezed the bridle in my hand. I had to open my eyes again before I stumbled and fell. I focused on something simple and calming. Dash's hooves made a thumping rhythm against the hard dirt we were walking on. As I focused, the thumping got louder and louder. Too loud. I heard him nicker deep and strong. *Wait, what? Dash's nicker isn't deep, it's squeaky.* My head whipped around as my eyes locked on a horse much bigger than Dash, a horse that was strong and brave and sometimes mean. But this time, like so many others, he had come back.

"Chance!" I screamed. He reared up, kicking at the air and bellowing loudly. When he came back down on all fours, he galloped the rest of the way up to us. Off in front of us ten feet rested a boulder about waist high. Chance tromped up to it and stood on the opposite side, looking at me. The tears streaming down my face now were joyful. I let out a noise between a laugh and a cry. Dash whinnied as if to ask Chance what took him so long. I could've sworn that Chance's response was sarcastic and hilarious.

Dash helped me hobble up to Chance, and I struggled up the rock and onto Chance's back. Chance looked back at me to make sure I was ready, then he looked back the way we'd come. For the first time, I realized that Rain and Pitch had come with Chance. Pitch called out a cry that couldn't have been interpreted as anything but a goodbye. Rain repeated the call, and then Chance replied to it with a sad call of his own. *He's choosing me. Even when he has the opportunity to live as a true mustang, free of all restraints, he's choosing me.* Rain and Pitch turned and trotted off into the dense woods we had come from and disappeared from view.

For a moment, I knew some of what Chance must have been feeling. I had found beautiful creatures I cared for and had to say goodbye to. It hurt to think that I might never see them again. But Chance had it worse. He had to say goodbye to *friends*. Chance stood still and watched the spot where the other horses had left for a few minutes, but then he turned to me, gave me a reassuring look, and started walking in the opposite direction.

Chance led Dash and me away from the woods and toward a hill in the distance. I didn't put the bridle back on him because it seemed rude, but it didn't matter. He led in a way where I couldn't help but trust he'd get us to our destination. What he'd done today I could never repay. His message was clear. *I will stay with you, my herd.*

33

Safe And Sound

I PROMISED MYSELF when I got home I would learn compass directions better. Chance and Dash were the navigators, not me. They were the only reason we made it back to the ranch. We traveled for several hours into the evening of the day. If I had to guess, and I did because I had left my watch in my tent the night of the wolf attack, I'd say we had about two hours of daylight left, which meant it was about 6:30. As the sun moved closer to the western horizon and the light began to fade slowly from the sky, we passed through the broken-down fence. We were now back within the boundaries of Cowboy Camp.

I began recognizing landmarks. We passed the spot where I collected berries while Jackie and Harley sat and watched. Then Chance took us past the first place Jackie and I met up with Harley and Kinzie. He continued on past these places farther in toward the Walden Creek Ranch headquarters, or at least in the direction I thought they were in. We were just about to ride up a big sloping hill when two riders came into view atop the rise. I could just barely recognize Jamie Lancaster and Mrs. Karen. They didn't see me at first because they were looking off to the side away from me.

"Hope Watkins," Jamie Lancaster hollered. Her voice cracked, like she'd been yelling at the top of her lungs all day.

"I'm over here," I croaked. My voice didn't get very high, and I tried again. "Here."

Both women caught the sound of my answer and looked to where the boys and I were. They kicked their horses into a gallop and barreled down the hill. Pulling up beside Chance and Dash, I was bombarded with questions.

"Where have you been?"

"Are you hurt?"

"Everyone's been worried sick."

"What happened?"

I didn't know which questions were asked by which woman, but I answered as best I could. "There were these wolves. I had to help Dash. And then these other horses. My leg's busted and so is my shoulder. I got lost. There's a fence down where animals can get in and out of this property." After I said all of this, I realized I probably didn't explain well, but both women must've gotten the gist of it with their "mom sense."

"Should've known it would've been you to get into trouble," Mrs. Karen mumbled under her breath. "Jamie, call Wyatt and tell him we're headed back. Call Mr. and Mrs. Watkins too." She then turned her attention fully to me. "Will you be able to manage the ride back?" Mrs. Karen asked me. She looked at me in a way that said she was both exasperated with me and maybe proud. I patted Chance's neck.

"Yes, I'll make it. Chance has been a lifesaver. He's the reason we got back here." Mrs. Karen looked like she wanted to ask me several questions but thought better of it.

"Let's get you back. You look awful, and I'm sure you're starving. The horses don't look as bad, but poor Dash looks like he just ran a marathon."

I looked down and realized she was right. I forgot more than I should that Dash had to work twice as hard to keep up because his legs were twice as short. But it didn't seem to be bothering him too much this time. He seemed to recognize Jamie Lancaster—she was one of the main ranch hands in charge of the miniature ponies—and knew he was headed back to a stall with lots of grain.

"What about the fence?" I asked her. I needed to make sure it was closed so Rain and Pitch wouldn't get stuck on the inside if they came this way.

"We'll make sure it gets fixed," she assured me.

The last leg of the trip back to Cowboy Camp was the easiest. Fifteen minutes out, Jamie Lancaster and Mrs. Karen had to use their flashlights, but the horses stayed calm and Chance seemed extra aware of my injured leg. The ranch was buzzing with movement when we got back, contrary to the fact that it was usually the time all the kids were in their cabins or surrounding the campfire.

I had so many people asking me what happened and how I was feeling and a dozen other things. There was an ambulance parked outside the main office, and when I rode in through the nearest gate, the paramedics were waiting and ready for me. They carefully and swiftly got me off Chance and onto a stretcher, then carted me to the ambulance and loaded me up. I pushed myself up onto my good elbow. When I started asking about the horses and what was happening, they only assured me everything would be okay and that I should relax. Before they shut the doors of the ambulance, I caught a glimpse of Kat looking after me worriedly and Austin putting Chance's bridle on him to lead him and Dash to the barn.

The doors closed, and the paramedics immediately started hooking me up to wires and an IV bag. I tried not to wince as one of the paramedics put the needle in my arm. I began to feel a little faint, and my palms got sweaty. Thankfully, the paramedic had a steady hand, and she got the needle in and stabilized on the first try. She talked to me about where we were going and assured me I was in good hands and my parents were on the way. I didn't hear much. It was all happening so fast now. I'd been in limbo for so many days that it was hard keeping up with everything happening.

I was vaguely aware of another paramedic harnessing my leg into a splint. The movements were a bit rough, but his motions were efficient and he attached the straps in a few quick strokes. The harness kept my leg from getting banged up before they examined it, I guessed. He looked up at me and smiled. That act helped to calm me. It reminded me of my dad. I leaned back on the stretcher and closed my eyes.

34

Tell Us Everything

I WOKE UP to the smell of disinfectant and the beeping of machines. I was lying on a white, twin-sized bed covered in thin white sheets in a room with plain white walls. I blinked several times at the harsh lighting. My eyes focused on a plaque hung on the wall outside of the room I laid in. It read, "Highlands Hospital: established 1987 Wolford, Oklahoma." I glanced to the right as I heard a squeal.

"You're awake," Kat gushed in the chair beside me. She got up quickly and bear-hugged me.

"Arm," I squeaked.

"Sorry," she said, releasing me quickly. "I got a little excited." I gingerly held my arm and grimaced.

"That's okay. I'm glad to see you too." I smiled. It was good to see Kat again. "How are the horses?" I asked her.

"Oh, they're fine. Resting up. Dash is catching up on some much-needed pampering. You know, what usually happens when horses leave civilization for a few days." I laughed. I could imagine Dash actually speaking to the people around him and telling them to massage his back and groom his mane and tail until there wasn't a hair out of place.

"What day is it?" I wondered aloud.

"July twenty-third," Kat replied. "You were out in the woods for ten days, Hope. You only got here last night."

Ten days? I thought. *I was stranded for five days on my own?* It both felt like too long a time and too short a time. I focused on Kat and realized she was about to burst.

"What?" I asked.

"You have to tell me everything," she squealed. She was practically jumping on the ceiling in anticipation. "Everyone has a different story on what happened to you. Some say you and Jackie got in a fight, and Jackie pushed you down a cliff. Others say you were chased by a bear or some other wild animal and—"

"If you don't slow down, Hope might go back to sleep and never wake up." I looked over to see the usual troublemaker smile plastered across Austin's face. He was sitting in the chair across the room. With his elbows on his knees and his fingers interlaced, he looked far more superior than Kat, even though he wasn't even quite two years older than either of us.

215

"I'm not going back to sleep," I assured him. "If I do, you might start treating my poor friend Kat like a daughter instead of a sister." I turned to Kat and stroked her arm fake protectively. "I won't let that happen to you, Kat. You mean too much to me."

"I wouldn't try acting like her father," Austin said, poorly sounding offended. He sat up straight and stuck out his chest in an exaggerated manner. "But I am older and smarter than Kat." He glanced at her and then looked and me. "And you."

"Oh, sure you are," I said, my words dripping with an overly dramatic flair. He chuckled good-naturedly.

"I'm glad you agree with me," he shot back.

I opened and closed my mouth without saying anything. *He got me there.* I turned to Kat and changed the subject. "Where are my parents?" I wasn't just trying to wipe the smirk off Austin's face but was also really curious. My parents should have been here.

"They're just out getting lunch," Kat said. "They stayed by you all night. But they had to leave about an hour ago before the nurses tried to offer them hospital food."

"We just got here," Austin continued. "Mom brought us. She came up here the same time as your parents. She wanted to be here in case anyone needed anything. And you know her. You're like a second daughter to her." At that moment, Mrs. Foster walked into the room.

"Oh, Hope. You're awake." She smiled widely and walked up and gave me a hug. Thankfully, though, she remembered that my right side was banged up and excluded it from the embrace. "Oh, I am so glad you're alright. Are you comfortable enough? Hungry?"

"I'm fine, Mrs. Liz," I said. "Just sore."

"Oh, I'm sure you are with your injuries."

"Which are?" I asked awkwardly.

"The kids didn't tell you?" Mrs. Liz asked, puzzled.

"Didn't get the time. She just woke up," Austin explained. He didn't seem to like that he had been referred to as a kid, but it was his mother. There wasn't much he could do.

"Oh, well, I have good news and bad news," Mrs. Liz said.

"Bad news first, please," I told her.

"Your leg is going to be in a cast for six weeks at least, and you can't ride for that time. Minimal walking is advised by your doctor and doing so needs to be done with crutches." She said this bluntly, ripping off the Band-Aid before I had a chance to brace myself. It was probably for the best.

"Six weeks?" I croaked, my voice dropping to how it had been when I screamed for hours on end for Chance and Dash.

"I'm sorry, Hope," Mrs. Liz said. She rubbed my back in a motherly way. "But the doctor also says that you can still be around the horses after a couple weeks. You just can't ride yet." I huffed and crossed my arms, then winced slightly with the movement of my right arm. It didn't hurt too awfully though. They must've put me on pain medicine.

"I don't need six weeks to get better." I sounded like a child, but I didn't care.

"Actually, you do," Mrs. Liz said firmly. "You don't have a concussion, and your arm is only strained and intensely bruised. You were slightly dehydrated and malnourished. We can thank God it wasn't worse." I looked at her, expecting the *but* to come. "But," *There it is.* "you did fracture your fibula pretty badly. It will take some time to heal."

"My what?"

"The smaller of the two bones in the bottom half of your leg, Dum Dum. It's used for balance," Austin said in his professor voice.

"Well, aren't you a walking encyclopedia," I muttered. *Six weeks? Fractured fibula?* This just got worse and worse.

"The bone didn't break the skin and was easily put back into place. They gave you a little bit of medicine while you slept so you wouldn't feel it," Mrs. Liz continued, unfazed. "You didn't have to have any bolts or screws in you. All in all, you're lucky. It could have been much worse."

For the first time, I looked down and saw the cast sticking out of the sheets slightly. It was propped up on several pillows like it was royalty. *Ugh.* I didn't like how comfortable it looked. I was not comfortable. I was not comfortable about being stuck on the ground for six weeks.

"Cheer up, sweetie. You're young, and soon, you'll be up on a horse again." Of course, she knew what I was thinking about. She kissed my head and said she needed to make a call to Mr. Foster. As she exited the room, I stared outside of it for no apparent reason. I didn't really see what I was looking at. I just replayed four words over and over in my head. *No riding. Six weeks. No riding. Six weeks. No riding.*

"Still waiting on that story about how you got abducted by aliens in the woods." Kat was great at distracting me, and she didn't fail this time either. I began the story and told Kat and Austin all about my adventure in the wilderness, minus, of course, the aliens.

There were a few points where Austin asked a clarifying question like "Who's Rain?" and "Why would you be stupid enough to climb onto a wild horse?" I didn't answer the second one, but I was surprised I had forgotten to mention Rain to him before this. *He's just jealous.*

I asked them to not tell any of the parents about the wild horses just yet. I planned on telling them, but there were only so many ways I could delicately say "I rode a wild horse to safety" without sounding like a lunatic. We were just finishing up our conversation when someone I didn't expect to see walked through the door of my hospital room.

Jackie held a box of chocolates in her hands. She had dark circles under her eyes she hadn't quite been able to hide with makeup. "Can I come in?" she asked.

"I guess," I said.

Jackie walked up to me quickly and gave me the chocolates. "These are for you. I'm sorry you got hurt."

"Thanks, but it wasn't your fault."

"Yes, it was," Jackie said. "You were alone for all that time by yourself because no one knew where you were."

"She's got a point," Kat said. I shot her a look. She was protective of me, but this was the humblest I had ever seen Jackie. I wasn't quite sure this was real.

"Sure, I could have used help scaring away the wolves. But it all happened so fast," I reasoned. "I don't blame you."

"Good," Jackie said, then tried again more confidently. "We're good then." A look of relief crossed her face. We both looked at each other for a minute and came to an unspoken agreement. We weren't friends really. I still didn't like that she had chased Rain. She still probably didn't like being around me. But neither of us wanted another enemy. I smiled. *She wouldn't be another Amy.*

Jackie headed back to the door. She turned just before leaving. "By the way, you should know that I was suspended from the Horsemanship Olympics. Same for Harley and Kinzie." I nodded. *I guess that means I'm out of the games too then.* No partner.

Jackie looked to the corner of the room and saw Austin. She immediately perked up. "Hi, Austin," she said in a sing-song voice. He turned pale and tried to sink into the chair and escape.

"Jackie, it's time to go," came a voice from the hall.

"Coming, Mom," she called. She waved goodbye to Austin and walked out. I was in a pretty good mood at the time, so I decided not to tease him.

Later, Mom and Dad came back with pizza. *Yes. My parents are the best.*

Over pizza—it wasn't Tony's Pizza Palace, but it was still pretty good—I told my story again. Mrs. Liz came back into the room right on time. It was going to take a little effort to tell the tale, so I was glad I would only have to do it once more today. I took a deep breath and delved into the story. Mom was horrified when I mentioned the wolves, and Dad didn't like my attitude very much when I talked about Jackie. Mrs. Liz winced in sympathy when I mentioned my struggles to get the apples out of the tree. I skipped over the part about Rain and told them about Chance and Dash helping me back instead.

They seemed to take it all pretty well. After we were done, my parents went to sign papers and get me checked out. Mrs. Liz left with Austin and Kat to take them back to camp. I wanted to go with them, but Mom said I couldn't leave until the doctors released me. I had to wait some more. Mom promised we would be on our way to the ranch soon as well. She said I wouldn't be staying long at camp though. I would have to go home to rest and miss the last six days of camp. *Ugh.*

35

Parting Ways

"FATHER, PLEASE," I reasoned. "I need to do this. I will never be satisfied here."

"I don't think this is a good idea. We need you," he whinnied. His voice was tired, as if the fight had almost left him.

"Father, I was born to guide a herd, but not this one." He needed to understand this. *The other mares think it would be better if an older mare led, and Magma will be the protector of this herd soon. He won't want me to be the lead mare either.* "This is the best option."

The General sighed and lowered his head for a moment. I hated to trouble him like this, but the past two weeks, I'd thought about nothing else. It had been driving me crazy. My father lifted his head and looked me in the eyes for a long moment. "You love him." It was not a question, not accusatory, just a fact he had noticed.

"He is my best friend," I replied simply.

He nodded. "Then I cannot keep you here," he nickered. "In fact, I should've seen it sooner." He pressed his head to mine, and the message was clear. It was a goodbye. *Go with him. I know you will be safe in his care.*

I pressed in closer to him, throwing my neck over his for just a minute and holding him. *Thank you, Father. This means so much to me.*

"You better visit on occasion," he whinnied firmly.

"But how will I find you?" I asked, backing away so that I could look him in the eyes.

"I have no intention of leaving this place. This is where I will stay for the remainder of my life," he nickered contentedly. "It is nice. You did a good job in finding it." He looked around him and watched a group of foals romp and play together. I could tell he was thinking about the days I had been that young, that small.

"I should've known you'd grow up to lead a life of your own," he whinnied. "It will suit you." He nodded behind me. I turned to see Fleetfoot standing a respectful distance off. He wasn't watching the foals, or the other mares, or even Magma. He looked straight at me. I nodded my head and neighed to show him my father said yes. He smiled, and I could see some of the tension in his shoulders ease up.

I turned back to my father as he whinnied, "Now go, before I change my mind." His smile was sad, but proud. He nipped at my mane playfully and nodded at me to go say goodbye to the others. I made my way through the herd, taking longer on some of the members than others. There were a few particularly tearful goodbyes. But then I was running up to Fleetfoot. He smiled and rubbed his nose against mine.

"Ready for another adventure?" he asked.

"With you, I wouldn't miss it." He turned, and together, we ran. We ran toward a place that started it all, a place where we were foals and could do anything, a place where we would start fresh. We ran so fast we flew, toward a new adventure.

36

Stretch Our Legs

SIX WEEKS, FIVE days, and a few odd hours later, it was finally time to get back in the saddle. My alarm clock screeched to life. Today I couldn't be bothered by the noise. Today was the day. I kicked the covers off and hobbled out of my bed. The cast itched like crazy, but I didn't notice. I was too busy speeding through getting ready for my doctor's appointment. I hastily threw my hair up in a ponytail and got dressed as fast as I could. I thumped down the stairs, and Mom came out of the kitchen, looking startled by the noise. When she saw me hopping around in excitement, she laughed.

"Looks like we better head out before you implode," she said.

It took about two hours to get to my appointment, wait our turn, get the cast off, and get back home. Mom had barely put the car in park before I tumbled out.

"Hope," Mom called. I turned to look at her, barely able to keep myself from walking backwards while I listened to her. "Just be careful, dear."

I raced to the barn next. Hearing barking, I glanced over to see my loyal buddy, Wolf, following at my heels. He had grown a lot over the summer, almost to his full height now. He still acted like a puppy on occasion and had been a big help in keeping me company the past month and a half. We caught up on all we had missed while I was at camp.

He tried not to let it show, but I could tell he had developed a "Momma's boy" attitude toward my mom while I was away. *But who could blame him?* Mom had spoiled him rotten. We raced together toward the barn. Wolf didn't get tired easily now, so he followed me around everywhere. He was going to come with Chance and me on our run today. We reached the pasture gate closest to the barn, and Chance was there waiting on us. We had bonded all over again in the past several weeks. It was amazing what constant grooming sessions would do to a friendship.

I swung the gate open and let Chance through and then closed the gate behind us. Our trio headed to the barn, and I got Chance tacked up quickly. I then grabbed his lead and headed toward the open plains behind our pastures. We passed Dash, who was busy munching on grass contentedly.

He looked up only long enough to whinny a good morning and then continued more important matters: eating. When we exited the last gate of my family's property, I halted Chance, and he turned to look at me knowingly. This was it. The doctor had warned me to take it easy at first because I might be a little rusty. I reached out and grabbed the saddle horn with my left hand and put my left foot in the stirrup. I bounced on my right foot one, two, three. With one single movement, I swung myself up onto Chance, feeling like a queen. It was just like riding a bike, just like breathing.

"Okay, Chance," I said, "let's ride."

We had so much fun that day. We walked and then ran and then trotted. We never stopped moving, though. We had too much pent-up energy. I spent much of the day reflecting on the end of Cowboy Camp. In the end, the camp was not going to get into any trouble for what happened to me. I had talked it over with my parents. It was an unlikely chain of events. Still, the wolves could be dealt with. The camp would take extra precaution to train students how to ward off the wolves and the ranchers would take preventative measures to drive the wolves away before students entered the open pastureland to begin with.

The competitive parts of the camp ended without many surprises. Jackie's update had been honest. Upon the discovery that Jackie, Harley and Kinzie had stayed together in the Trail Trials for much of the time they were in the woods, they were disqualified from the competition before the Horsemanship Olympics even took place. It hurt to know Jackie was out of the contest. We hadn't been actual friends, but I had begun to believe we stood a shot at winning. But there was also the other problem, I was a cripple. Whether Jackie had been disqualified or not, there was no winning the competition for us.

In the end, the Trail Trial winners were no underdogs. The pair who stayed out the longest was Austin and Zeke with Danny and her partner coming in at a close second. I had kicked Austin in the shin when I realized he had been hiding his victory from me at the hospital.

Danny's team had to come in because her partner apparently had an allergic reaction to a bee sting. She was fine after a quick trip to the doctor's office. Technically speaking, I had stayed out two days longer than anyone else but that didn't count because I was MIA.

The last thing that happened at Cowboy Camp, however, was a complete surprise to everyone. Once the scores from the Trail Trial, the Horsemanship Olympics—which included all of the skills we'd learned like roping and barrel racing—and total camp teamwork were tallied, the winners were Kat and Tiffany. I was so happy for them. Sure, it bummed me out that I didn't get a shot at it, but I was truly happy for them. And really, the adventure I had with Rain, Pitch, Chance, and Dash was *way* better. I'd be back to the Walden Creek Ranch Cowboy Camp again next year, but the days in those woods couldn't be replaced.

Kat said the last evening campfire was full of stories and goodbyes. It was all really sweet and wonderful, though I wouldn't know personally, since I wasn't there to see it. Friends were sharing phone numbers and promising to keep in touch. Kat and Tiffany actually had talked a bit since camp ended. They formed an unlikely friendship. I had a few opportunities to hang out with Tiffany after camp, and I had to agree with Kat that she was pretty cool.

The sun was running away from us. The shadows were creeping in. "We better head back, Chance," I said, patting his neck. I tugged on his reins to turn him back toward the house, but he froze and pricked his ears in the opposite direction. He turned his head to look and then turned his body fully around. "Chance, you big goof, what are you—" I stopped short. I held my breath, wanting to freeze time. *How long have they been following us?*

The dappled-gray mare pranced up beside us and a stallion, dark as night, followed. They didn't come close. They were still a good thirty feet away, but they came.

"Rain, Pitch, you found us," I whispered. It seemed too surreal a moment to yell for joy. Seeing them again should have been nearly impossible, but the fact that they were here meant they came looking. They cantered around us. Chance stayed uncharacteristically quiet, and so did Wolf. It was like they knew this moment was magical.

Rain came for a reason. *What is it, though? Does she want to show me something?* Pitch and Rain circled around us. So close, but never too close. Pitch stayed farther away but kept a careful watch on Rain. *He's protecting her.* I realized. *Rain joined Pitch. They're starting a herd.* I had only guessed last time I saw them, but this was proof. They both looked so happy and carefree, healthy and strong. They seemed like a perfect match to me.

I could imagine what it would be like in several years, and it warmed my heart that Rain would trust me to see the beginning of their new herd. All of these thoughts came to a close when Pitch swung in between us and Rain. He shook his head at us and then pushed in closer to Rain, directing her away and up the slope. The message was easy to interpret. *It's time to go now.*

Rain looked back at me briefly before she galloped away with Pitch. They ran across the plains as fast as only true mustangs could, blazing effortlessly across the land. Rain and Pitch only stopped when they reached the crest of a hill that would take them out of our sight. It happened quickly, so quickly that I'd later think I'd dreamed it. Rain turned and looked back at us. She reared up, front legs reaching for the heavens. Her cry carried on the wind, back toward us. By the time I could hear it, it was a whisper, and Rain was already out of sight. It spoke of a vow or oath, a promise to see each other again, someday.

GLOSSARY

Amy Turner: Hope's "summer sister" who stole Chance and got Hope grounded for a whole summer.

Austin Foster: Kat's older brother and a hard worker who loves to tease Hope. He has lots of girls falling for him, but he gets embarrassed when it's mentioned.

Banjo: Mrs. Foster's bay gelding.

Blitzen: Austin's big, black-and-white pinto gelding.

Butterscotch: A filly at Watkins' Wild Ranch.

Calypso: Kat's coal-black mare. She is usually nervous until someone cheers her name.

Chance: Hope's buckskin gelding mustang, Sugar's foal, acts like a dog sometimes and is very hyper. He's a ham.

Chloe: A nine-year-old Hope meets at Cowboy Camp who is friends with Zoe and sunscreens by the can.

Cowboy Camp: A summer camp held at Walden Creek Ranch in Wolford, Oklahoma.

Danny Taylor: An expert barrel racer who is competitive but a good sport.

Dash: Hope's black Shetland pony she received as a six-year-old. She rode him before Chance. He is nicknamed Fuzzy by Jackie.

Fleetfoot: A two-year-old stallion with a pitch-black coat, said to have died in an earthquake (earthshake) as a yearling. His human name is Pitch and was named that by Hope because of his dark coat.

Foreman: Helps run the Foster's cattle ranch and is in his late forties.

Harley Young: A part of The Diva Posse and paired with Kinzie in the Horsemanship Olympics.

Highlands Hospital: The place where Hope is treated.

Hope's Grandpa: Told Hope about the "heartbeat of the ranch."

Hope Watkins: Lives at Watkins' Wild Ranch with her Mom and Dad and their horses, is fourteen, and paired with Jackie King in the Horsemanship Olympics.

Jackie King: The competitive leader of The Diva Posse. She is paired with Hope in the Horsemanship Olympics.

Jamie Lancaster: One of Cowboy Camp's leaders and is in charge of the miniature ponies.

Joe: Seventeen-year-old ranch hand at the Foster's cattle ranch. He has pepper-red hair.

John Foster: The husband of Mrs. Liz, father of Kat and Austin, co-owner of the Foster cattle ranch, and is forty years old.

Katherine (Kat) Foster: Hope's best friend and comrade in all of her adventures and a fourteen-year-old tomboy.

Kinzie: Paired with Harley in the Horsemanship Olympics, is not good with directions, and doesn't care much about following rules.

Magma: A two-year-old dark buckskin with a coat the color of molten gold. The stallion who will take over The General's herd. His human name is Spirit because he bears a striking resemblance to the animated character in *Spirit: Stallion of the Cimarron*.

Moonlace: A mare who The General took in. She had Fleetfoot a week after she was taken in by the stallion and his herd.

Mrs. Elizabeth (Liz) Foster: The wife of John, mother of Kat and Austin, co-owner of the Foster cattle ranch, and is in her late thirties.

Mrs. Karen: The stern barrel racing instructor at Cowboy Camp. She has a good sense of humor when she decides to show it.

Mrs. Watkins (Mom): Wife to Mr. Watkins, mother of Hope, and co-owner of Watkins' Wild Ranch.

Mr. Watkins (Dad): Husband to Mrs. Watkins, father of Hope, and co-owner of Watkins' Wild Ranch.

Paco: A big paint stallion who thinks he's all that but gets scared away from Skytears by Fleetfoot.

Riley: Hope's cousin, and the one who mentions Cowboy Camp to Mrs. Watkins. She went to camp the year before Hope as a senior.

Skytears: A dappled-gray, wild mustang mare befriended by Hope. She is the unofficial lead mare of The General's band until she leaves to join Fleetfoot. Her human name is Raindancer.

Staccato: Danny's twelve-year-old, bay, gelding quarter horse.

Sugar: Chance's mom and a mare at Watkins' Wild Ranch who loves sugar.

Sugarfoot: Jackie's palomino mare.

Sundancer: Joe's pepper-red mare.

The Diva Posse: Jackie King, Tiffany Stratton, and Harley Young.

The General: The dark buckskin leader of a band of mustangs.

The General's Band: A herd consisting of six mares, four foals, Magma, Skytears, and The General. The herd is led by The General, but soon Magma, with Skytears as the current lead mare.

Tiffany Stratton: A shy pushover. She is the nicest in The Diva Posse and is partnered with Kat in the Horsemanship Olympics.

Walden Creek Ranch: The ranch owned by Wyatt Walden in Wolford, Oklahoma, and is where Cowboy Camp is held.

Watkins' Wild Ranch: The ranch where Hope and her family live.

Wolf: Hope's blue merle Australian Shepherd puppy.

Wyatt Walden: The owner of Walden Creek Ranch and leader of Cowboy Camp, located at his ranch in Wolford, Oklahoma.

Zeke: Austin's partner in the Olympics.

Zoe: A nine-year-old Hope meets at Cowboy Camp who is friends with Chloe.

ACKNOWLEDGMENTS

This book did not come together overnight. In fact, it has taken me about eight years to complete. Along the way, I had so many wonderful people ask me about what I was writing. Slowly, painstakingly slowly, it began to come together. Without these people showing an interest, *Saving Hope* might not have made it to publishing.

Not only did I have so many people showing an interest in my work—friends, relatives, mentors—I had several wonderful people who read my early drafts and helped me to hone in the story. To those people, you are incredible.

Mom, this book should have your name on it too after how many times I called you to talk through things. You read the book, cover to cover, more than anyone else besides me. Sometimes I was worried I was annoying you with all my questions, and maybe I was, but you always listened and gave me solid advice. I can't thank you enough.

Cindy Ray Hale, you are a book saver. As my editor, you helped me smooth over the cracks in my writing. You understand what it's like to have a story you want the world to read but know it will take many, many drafts to make it readable. Though I haven't known you a long time, I am so glad you came into my life when you did. You caught many of the mistakes I had become blind to and helped me raise the stakes of my story so it would have a greater impact on my readers.

Lastly, I want to recognize my amazing LifeRich Publishing team. These incredible people were instrumental in the final stages of this project. They took the story I had and helped me get it to readers.

I could fill up several more pages listing all the people who helped get this book into readers' hands, but I am pretty sure I would still forget to thank someone. If you think I have forgotten about you, I have not. Please know your encouragement means a great deal to me now, and every day, *Saving Hope* will be in the hands of people who will love the story just as much as I do.

ABOUT THE AUTHOR

S.J. Palmer grew up in southern Oklahoma on a small farm with her dad, mom, and five siblings. After being homeschooled, she attended Oklahoma State University to sharpen her writing skills.

Until Palmer was two, her parents thought she might be mute. But since she started talking, she has never stopped. As she grew up, her talking turned to reading and then to writing. She has a never-ending list of books to read and write. For more about her and her writing, visit https://authorsjpalmer.wixsite.com/creative-writing.

CPSIA information can be obtained
at www.ICGtesting.com
Printed in the USA
LVHW101755110422
715892LV00003B/448